PLANET DEAD

SYLVESTER BARZEY

To Leanna,
Congratulations on
winning a one way
ticket into Planet Dead
Enjoy!!

I want to thank
My mother for giving me life.
My wife for giving me hope.
My son for giving me purpose.
& God for everything else.

CONTENTS

FOREWORD

PLANET DEAD

PLANET DEAD FOREWORD
BY CHRISTOPHER ARTINIAN

Sylvester and I started our respective journeys into the world of Indie publishing at about the same time. When you take those first steps, it is difficult to find a firm footing, and you can have all the ambition in the world, but you can never be sure of where you will end up. You can only aim and hope.

We bumped into each other a few times on social media and I was always impressed by a number of aspects of Sylvester's character. I'm old fashioned in many respects, and the first thing that endeared him to me was the fact that he was just such a good and decent man. He was always very polite and very humble. He always took the time to ask how things were going regardless of what was going on in his life, and this was the reason we became friends.

As time went on and I got to know more about him I became aware of just how focussed and how dedicated he was to his craft. The world of post-apocalyptic zombie fiction is vastly populated and my reading list is always growing longer rather than shorter; so when I let a book jump the queue it is with good reason. I picked up a copy of Planet Dead and was hooked from the first few pages. Sylvester has a real talent for creating a feel for an environment without reams of exposition. I hate spoilers, so don't expect to see any here, but I can tell you that I loved the development and the aspect of the relationships that are cultivated in this book. The uneasy beginning between Catherine and Sue is cleverly constructed to set the tone of the entire story. It reveals enough of their respective characters, temperaments and philosophies to leave you yearning to find out more, and this is a real skill to display in the first few pages of a book.

There is a beautiful mix of action and emotion in this work. It is authentic, humorous and exciting and in Catherine Briggs, Sylvester has created an enduring and powerful leading character that makes the reader cry out for more. It's not an easy feat in any literary genre but the ZOMPOC field in particular is a harsh proving ground for likable and memorable heroes and heroines.

I felt Sylvester struck a real blow with this debut novel. It is very hard to show the best aspects of your writing on your very first outing, but all the elements are present here, and you finish the book wondering just how the quality, tempo and drama can be matched in a sequel.

After reading Planet Dead: Bloodthirsty, I kept an eye on Sylvester's career as I felt sure this would just be the start of something big, and I was right. Sylvester has gone from strength to strength with more verve and heart than most. He has developed not just his writing, but other skills specifically to embrace the power of technology, the internet and social media like no other author I have met.

The longer you know him, the more you realize you don't know him. There are so many facets to this man that you just wonder what he will get up to next. He has created a striking brand and presence with some amazing video and graphic packages and, his commitment to the genre and the Indie movement is real and sincere. He has helped to promote countless other authors at no profit to himself simply because he can and this is why he encapsulates the true essence of Indie.

It is hard to enter into the zompoc world on any social media site without seeing his name because there is a real buzz about this great new talent. 2017 was the start of the trail for Sylvester with Planet Dead: Bloodthirsty. Catherine Briggs is something special and I can't wait to find out where the journey goes for him and her from here on in.

What I do know is that in this rich and varied genre there are some authors who can make you raise an eyebrow. Sylvester is one such writer. He has a real spark and drive that is infectious. It is present in his writing, and it is present in his life.

So, without further ado, I would like to welcome you to the Sylvester Barzey universe, and more specifically, to Planet Dead. Enjoy!

If you enjoy this book:

Leave a review.
Tell a friend.
Visit my website
Thank You

PROLOGUE

"Good evening America." The Vice President's voice came out strong and clear through the sound system of the press room. The red, white and blue flag stood proudly behind him. Everything was polished and dressed up to look it's best. They took their time to set this up, which was surprising. This press conference wasn't about border control, gun control, or any other form of control. No this was the total opposite, this was about anarchy. A wave of madness took to the streets of America and throughout the media there was an unanswered question that kept being raised: where is the president?

"Tonight, you might be wondering why I'm speaking to you and not our fair President. Many of you might have heard stories about his health. Many of you have expressed your concerns about his well-being. Well, both he and I would like to thank you for your thoughts and prayers, but, despite what you fine people of the media would like the American people to believe, our leader is in good health."

Fake news was a real thing. Some broadcasters were paid big money to chase pointless topics or to leave out a story or two. No one talked about the missing girls in Africa. Woody Allen got his stories pre-screened for years. Fake news was a real thing, but this wasn't fake news, this wasn't even news. A virus was quickly taking over countries all around the world, this was reality. Now, after months of swearing how strong and protected our nation was, it was finally here.

"The President was rushed out of the city before the outbreak and is being held in an undisclosed location until we have a better understanding of what is going on. Our leader will return, and he will see us through this dark hour."

Russia was the first to fall. No one understood what was happening; one minute people were getting sick, the next people were dying. But they didn't stay dead. Russia wasn't prepared; no one was.

"Not much is known about this virus or how it got on American soil. We can go back and forth for days about who's to blame for our position at the moment. I could take the low ground and say this is exactly why we wanted to fully close our borders to the outside world. I could bring up that this is the exact reason why we built the wall in the first place, but I'm not that kind of person."

The Southern Grand, more commonly referred to as the wall, was the one campaign promise that was fulfilled by our fearless leader. A technological marvel that runs from coast to coast blocking America off from Mexico and the rest of South America. An invisible electrical field, which was solar powered of all things, was meant to be the saving grace of America. Now it was the saving grace of South America, keeping the infected at bay.

"What I will address are the facts that we do know. At approximately 0900 hours, a tourist group entered the White House. One of the said tourists abandoned the tour group and was apprehended on her way to the Oval Office."

The world lost all communication with the UK two months

ago. People started getting scared, and when people get scared, they get violent. People who claimed to have America's best interest at heart were rounding up everyone they felt wasn't' American enough. Green card holders, immigrants, and anyone that couldn't prove, without a shadow of a doubt, that they were born in America were at risk. That two-week period was poetically named The Hunt by the administration.

"As we waited for the proper authorities to remove the woman, the Secret Service was informed she was a person of interest in an ongoing investigation being done by the CDC. The woman was then escorted out of the building where her counterparts opened fire, killing two guards. The reports that those two guards returned after death or that the woman was a carrier of the infection are beyond false. There have been reports of the infection in the D.C area, but our country's best scientists are conducting research to fully understand what we're dealing with. Be assured, we have this under control. Now, I'll take a few questions, yes you..."

This was not a press conference about control because control, and the illusion of it, was far more dead than anything else in this new era.

"I didn't say the President was rushed out of the city before the outbreak, you must have misheard me. Next question..."

This era was one of blood.

"We haven't heard any reports about the woman being a United States employee, and to even suggest that an American would attack our country like that is just sinful."

An era of hate.

"Listen, what is happening around the world doesn't need to happen to us. We are Americans! We are smart. We are strong, and we're not gonna let something like a virus turn our nation upside down!"

An era of fear and...

"Next question, you in the back..."

"What's wrong with him? What's wrong with him?"

"Shoot him! Shoot him goddamnit!"

"I don't care how many people are watching! Get me the hell out of here and kill that son of a-"

An era of the dead.

After that broadcast D.C went dark.

People call it the last words of a dying nation.

It was our first look into a new order of life.

It was our first look into...

Planet Dead.

1

THEY'RE COMING TO GET YOU

PLANET DEAD

"*Mommy.*"

The faint word was almost overlooked and ignored like the passing buzz of a fly. Then that faint buzz transformed into a thunderous roar that broke through the forceful southern winds. "Mommy!"

A head shot up above the tall grass looking for lips that cried out for her. From side to side she searched until her eyes finally found him. Her little boy was standing on the hilltop, his small hands cupping his mouth as he fought to scream into the wind, "Mommy!"

Like helpful arms, his voice was pulling her to her feet. Breaking her free from the fog that had taken over her mind. Clear droplets of sweat ran down his cheek and along his neck. She could see that, along with the dirt and blood that stained his face.

"Jordan?" she said softly. Her mind was tossed into a maze of questions. *Why was he here? Where was here?* But the most chilling of all questions was, *whose blood was on his face?* "JOR-DAN!" she screamed. Every muscle in her body tightened and readied to race toward her son, but, before she could take her first step, she felt a cool hand run along her bare shoulder.

"He's all right, Cat. He's just playing games," said a calming and commanding voice. She stood still, her skin softened as the gusting winds died down into a soft summer breeze. Her eyes were still fixed on her son; who was screaming as if he were sending every bit of air in his lungs out to deliver his message, but as the cool hand slowly made its way from her sun-kissed shoulders to the spot where her neck and her jaw line met, the cries of the little boy began to fade back into a faint buzz and her eyes closed, "Boys will be boys, right?" The hairs on her neck spiked up and her body tingled as his words whispered into her ear. The waves of emotions running through her became still. He leaned into her and his lips brushed her ear as he whispered, "Catherine."

Catherine's eyes opened with a smile, but it dropped at the sight of the tears in her son's eyes. Jordan's mouth was wide open, releasing a word that was far clearer than any word Catherine had heard in years, "Run!"

Before she could react, the soft calming hand resting on her skin turned into a vice grip, pulling Catherine down into the tall grass. Towering over her was the monster she once called her husband. The once golden, brown skin that she had kissed and cared for was now a dark, grayish black. His white eyes scanned over her, and for a moment, she swore he was smiling. Hands began springing up from the ground, latching onto her body. Nails and bones tore into her flesh, exposing blood and bright red meat. Her lips parted but only a deep gargle of her throat could be heard. The hands viciously dragged Catherine into the darkness of the earth. Her zombie husband leaned down until they were face to bloody face, "Run, Catherine!"

Catherine shot up screaming. She kicked and punched, but as her eyes took in the grim view of the rundown bedroom and the sleeping bag that had been flung to the floor, it was clear it was all a dream. Catherine sat still, letting her racing heart calm itself. Her eyes scanned the room until they spotted the curtains dancing in the cool night's breeze.

"Fuck." She pulled the window down quickly, but carefully enough to avoid slamming it closed. It was wise to avoid loud sounds these days; loud sounds brought attention, and attention was sure to get you killed.

Gazing out into the darkness of the night, Catherine pulled her hair back into a ponytail. She was toned; trading tan boots for courtroom high heels hadn't 'kept her from training every day. The only thing that slowed down her workouts was the damn apocalypse. Catherine couldn't justify going for a jog with flesh eating monsters on every corner.

Her skin was far darker than its normal caramel brown, covered with cuts and bruises from her newfound life on the bottom of the food chain. Catherine rested her head on the window, before turning around and snatching up the shotgun that rested by the bed. The double-barreled beauty was the only object she held near and dear to her heart, well that and the double-edged knife she kept hidden in her boot.

Making her way through the darkness of the house, Catherine found herself on the staircase. Photos lined the wall in a cute descending pattern. A happy family in each dusty frame stared back at her. It had been days since she saw another living person. Which, on one hand was a blessing.

Catherine was free to travel without worry, without having to care for anyone's needs or wonder if they'll make it through the night. It took up too much brain power worrying about others and she needed her wits about her to make it through the coming days.

Yet, there was something to be said about having a partner. Someone that could share in the pain. Someone that could pull you out of the darkness from time to time.

Catherine's footsteps echoed throughout the house as she

made her way down the staircase, performing the normal nightly checks. Walking into the kitchen, she gave it the standard once over; the windows were boarded up, *check*. Supplies were broken down into daily rations on the counter, *check*. Shotgun ammo right next to the escape bag on the kitchen table for a quick exit, *check*.

Her fingers stroked the wooden boards covering the window. She smiled, but her peace of mind rapidly faded when a rapid pounding started shaking the front door. Catherine stared at the old wood, not wanting to move because moving toward it would make it real. She stood there, listening to the frantic pounding coming from beyond the wood.

"Hello!" The pounded grew louder as it accompanied the shrieking voice that came from beyond the door. "Is anyone in there? Oh God!"

It was the scream of a young woman, her voice and fist growing louder. The woman banged on the door for her life as she prayed she hadn't imagined the dim light in the distance, that it wasn't some kind of mirage of safety that her mind created. She slammed her hands into the wooden door. She glanced over her shoulder, an action that caused her heart to start pounding louder than her hands. A mix of sweat and tears covered her rose-pink face as she parted her lips to scream out once again.

"PLEASE! OPEN THE DOOR! GOD! PLEASE!"

The pleading wasn't only grabbing Catherine's attention but also the attention of her pursuers.

The butt of the shotgun was forced tightly into Catherine's shoulder pocket. Cautiously, she made her way over toward the door. Her heart was still, no panic could be seen on her face. All that stood out was the look of a student, studying her surroundings and coming up with her next course of action.

Catherine was a product of war, one fought over in countries most couldn't pronounce for reasons most wouldn't believe. She learned like the good student she was and remembered everything, never hoping to have to use any of it again, but fate had other plans. War was her class and, as she listened to the screaming and the pounding, she knew class was in session.

Now, she could walk away and ignore it all, but there would be no telling how many of those things would be outside in the morning. She could open the door and put an end to the screams with one fast pull of the trigger, but what would that make her? Her left hand came off the pump-action shotgun and she placed it on the lock of the door. She could have done a number of things, but there was really only one action she could live with in the morning. "Who are you?"

The young woman stopped her pounding, and her tear-filled eyes were pulled up from the ground by the sound of Catherine's voice. The woman had given up. She had come to terms with the end. She said her internal goodbyes to about a thousand people before Catherine's voice broke through the door with its gust of hope and it's peculiar question. The girl had ignored a few knocks since the dead had risen but never one followed by pleads for help.

"Who am I?" The young woman paused. Then she started to pound and kick at the door harder than before. Bright red blood poured from her bare knuckles. "Who fucking cares?! Just open the door!"

A loud splash caused her to go still, she fearfully glanced over her shoulder, as a bucket fell into the dark waters of a nearby well. Two haunting figures slowly crept toward her in the distance. The young woman once again pounded and kicked at the door for dear life.

"Please! PLEASE!"

Catherine turned the lock on the door and pulled it open, only to have the young woman rush past her into the safety of the house. Catherine's fear of never being able to forgive herself won out over the fear of death. Now it was them against the monsters.

Hustling through the darkness were the figures, breaking through the high blades of grass on the lawn. Twisted, broken, and smelling like microwaved shit; they started to become clearer to Catherine. One had no lips, just bloodstained teeth that chomped as he dragged his left leg along the grass. He seemed to have been infected for some time now; his skin was rotting, and maggots were swarming along his bloody flesh. The other was newly infected. His clothing wasn't dirty compared to his counterpart and his face looked the same as any other normal person, aside from his gray, pale eyes and the blood running down his chest, from the large pulsating wound on his chest.

His look wasn't the only thing that gave his time of infection away. No, his movement did that as well; he wasn't slow-moving or stumbling. The man walked at a brisk pace compared to the other. Their moans grew louder as they came closer to the house.

"What are you waiting for?" The young woman screamed.

The zombies' heads snapped up violently. Their gray eyes focused on Catherine. The newly infected zombie's walk turned into a full-on sprint, cutting through the high grass. The other dragged his leg along so fast and with such force, it seemed as if it would rip off.

"Fuck this!" the woman shouted. She grabbed the door, only to see Catherine's black combat boot slam into it, forcing the door out of the woman's grasp.

"Touch that door and I'll blow your damn head off!" Catherine's icy tone caused the young woman to take two cautious steps back.

The woman's eyes darted rapidly from the monsters moving briskly through the night to what she presumed to be a crazed shut-in standing with her shotgun at the ready.

Catherine didn't pay the woman's panicked glares any mind; she made no attempts to reassure her of their safety. She never broke her focus from the oncoming threat that revealed itself under the glow of the moonlight. The young woman's skin tightened, and her mouth grew dry as the moans of the zombies grew louder. Death was quickly approaching.

Catherine cocked back the pump handle, sending a large red round into the barrel. She closed her eyes for a moment and released a breath she didn't realize she had been holding. She pulled the trigger, sending a shockwave into her shoulder. Their ears rang from the barrel releasing an echoing **BOOM.**

The newest zombie or as Catherine called them, the half-baked, flew back, limbs flailing through the air like a rag doll until he collided with the ground. However, just as fast as his body hit the ground, he popped back up, leaping toward the steps. Catherine pumped back the rifle again, sending an empty cartridge descending to the ground and a new round into the chamber. The trigger pulled back and another roaring **BOOM** was heard.

The young woman covered her ears. "What the hell is wrong with you?" she shouted. The duo watched the head of the slower, fully cooked, zombie exploded from the shot.

A quick pump and Catherine sent another cartridge flying, but this time, nothing was there to replace it. The sound of the trigger's useless click sent a chill down her spine. The half-baked zombie was still running full sprint toward the door. Catherine's eyes widened, and her hand went to her pockets but came up with empty hopes and dreams.

"Fuck, fuck, FUCK!" Catherine spun her head toward the young woman and started to bark orders at her as if she was back on base and caught the woman asleep on guard duty, "I need bullets! Hurry up!" The woman dashed toward the living room, "No! The red box in the kitchen!"

The half-baked zombie was getting closer and closer to the

steps, thick red foaming blood escaping from his lips. He was just like the others, a mindless killing machine whose only concern was where his next bite came from. Catherine had no plans of dying anytime soon, but fate and Catherine were never on the same page.

The young girl doubled back around, her eyes glancing through the open door. She could see the ugly figure racing toward Catherine. Everything felt slow in that moment, and for the first time she could see what she was running from. It wasn't just a photo on the internet, it wasn't some grainy video on the TV, or sounds coming from beyond a locked door. It was real, and it was moments away from ending her life. She bolted into the kitchen and pulled open cabinet doors. She raced around the room until her eyes rested on a small red box on the table. She grabbed it and dashed toward the doorway once again. She tossed the box at the woman, who snatched it out of the air. Catherine's fingers dug into the box and pulled out a red shell. She dropped the box to the ground and reloaded.

She quickly raised the shotgun, pressing her cheek against the butt-stock, her eyes were locked in a stare down with the monster, it was looking right at her with those dead gray eyes. There was no blinking, no moving, just her staring at the monster and it staring right back into her soul. Her fingers were sweating as they pressed hard against the metal.

A cool wind blew and caused the door to smack into the wall, with that one sound the being took a leap forward, landing him at the top of the house steps. She pumped the handle and the shell leaped into the barrel. She pulled the trigger. Cold blood flew through the night and onto her face as she tightly closed her eyes and mouth.

The headless body fell to the floor and the young girl stood there looking at the sight.

"Nasty," the girl said softly.

"Damn it. I hope I didn't get any in my eyes!" Catherine said as she pulled up her shirt and started cleaning off her face. Walking past the young girl, Catherine made her way up the steps as she sharply let out, "Close the door!"

The young girl slammed the door shut, and her fingers quickly twisted the metal to lock the door. She rested her forehead on the chipped paint of the door. She was alive, and she was safe. Two things she never thought she would be just a few short minutes ago. The girl turned around slowly, her head hanging low as she forced herself to look up at her hero and mumble the words: "Thank you."

Catherine came to a full stop on the staircase. She didn't turn around to face the young girl, she simply asked softly, "For what?"

"For saving me," the girl replied.

Rolling her eyes slightly, Catherine turned around and smiled. She had rubbed most of the blood from her face and into her white torn tee-shirt, but a dark red stain remained on her caramel skin. She stood in the middle of the staircase with her black bra tightly strapped to her chest like a plate of armor, she held her shotgun in her hands. Taking a few slow steps down as she said,

"You make it sound like I had a choice in the matter. If they would have gotten you, then you would have turned, and there would have been one extra freak to put down."

The young girl nodded as she walked toward the steps.

"Yeah, but still, I- " she said but was quickly cut off when Catherine pointed the shotgun into the girl's face.

The young girl's eyes fixed on the dark hole that led into the barrel of the shotgun, her hands slowly moving up. They trembled in the air just above her shoulders. That feeling of her heart leaping out of her chest was back again, but this time, she wasn't running from the infected, that was before, and this time she thought she was safe.

"Don't come any closer," the bloodstained woman sharply

demanded, causing the young girl to take a step back. She survived all of that madness only to be unlucky enough to lock herself in an old house with a crazy person.

The young girl swallowed hard, trying to get the dryness out of her mouth. "What the hell, lady?" She hoped she sounded unafraid. She knew, in that moment, she had made a mistake. Her eyes burned with tears and she knew that all the bloodstained woman saw was a weak intruder who almost got them both killed. The young girl continued taking steps back as Catherine walked down the steps, never lowering her shotgun from the middle of the girl's face. She backed up until she felt the locked door pressed up against her.

There was nowhere to run, so she stared back into the darkness of the shotgun barrel. It was an odd thing to go from feeling like you're going to die, to being saved, to be right back at death's door once again. An odd feeling that she wouldn't wish on her worst enemies.

"You stay down here," Catherine said softly as she pulled back the pump handle of the shotgun one more time, sending a red shell flying through the air once again. She drove her point home by pushing the hot barrel into the bare-skinned shoulder of the girl as she continued, "and you leave in the morning."

Questioning a crazy person was never a good idea, even before the world went to hell. It could lead to yelling, fighting, shit being thrown at your face, but with the world coming to an end and everyone grabbing every form of firearms they could get their hands on, questioning a crazy person now could only lead to one outcome: death. Even with that thought in mind, the shock of being cast out into the madness in the morning once again prevented the girl from holding her tongue. The young girl's eyebrows quickly went up and her hands dropped, pushing the shotgun away from her shoulder.

"What's your deal, lady? It's not like I'm one of those damn things out there! I'm human!" the girl screamed into Catherine's face.

The woman nodded as she leaned over with her shotgun to pick up the box of ammo. She casually reloaded the weapon as she said, "Yeah, well, that's just as bad in my book."

She held the weapon in one hand, and with one sharp, swift motion, she pulled back the pump handle and reloaded the weapon with one hand. She turned around and, once again, started back up the steps.

The young girl shook her head and watched as the woman made her way up the stairs. When she turned the corner of the staircase and her last step was out of view, the girl's hands flew to her face, trying to push her tears back into her eyes. She then bit down on her lip as she placed her hand over her chest, trying to slow the pounding. The whole house was dark; she could hardly see in front of her. The light of the moon came through the cracks and spaces of the boarded-up windows. The girl moved toward the staircase and peeked her head around as far as she could without putting her foot on the steps.

When she thought she was in the clear, she took a step back and looked around at her new surroundings. She started toward one of the gaps between the boards that let in a peaceful, bright glow of moonlight and placed her eye against it. She felt the cool air from the outside run along her cheek. She could see the dark path that she ran from the woods to the house; her legs were still burning from the deadly foot race.

The young girl turned away from the window. She wanted to leave the outside where it was, even if it was just for the night. She strolled around the living room, running her hand lightly along the fireplace. When she pulled it back, her fingers were covered in dust, and a long spider's web had wrapped itself around her hand. She shook her hand frantically.

The girl let out a childlike whine and ran her hand up and down on her blue jean shorts. Spiders, shotguns, and zombies made their way to the top five list of things she hated, right behind her ex-boyfriend and circus clowns. She sighed as she looked down at the fireplace, she got down to her knees on the dusty floor and started to move the logs about, causing black soot to kick up into the air. She waved her hand back and forth and coughed.

"Someone needs some cleaning lessons," she softly sang.

Pulling out a lighter from her front pocket, she held it to the dark wood, and some balled up paper that had been sitting there forever, most likely left by another poor soul who just wanted to see through the darkness of the world. Odds were that soul got shot for walking up the stairs. The thought of that soul losing their life like that was heartbreaking, but oddly funny to the girl, who let out a small laugh. Soon a small fire started that slowly lit up the room. She sat there looking at it, letting the flames fill up her eyes. She was safe now, as safe as she could ever be in this new world.

""What the hell do you think you're doing?"" The voice came from behind the girl, causing her to shoot up and bang her head on the dusty fireplace mantle.

The girl's hand went over the top of her head and shouted, "Damn it!" The girl stood up, rubbing her head as she turned fully around to face the crazy woman. "I was just..." The girl's hand fell to her side. She looked around and said softly, "There are no lights in this place; I can't see a thing."

Catherine had a towel around her neck and a new black tight sleeveless shirt on, well-worn and with some rips, but far fewer than the balled up, bloodied one she once had. She started toward the fireplace. Her hair was wet and sticking to the back of her neck. "That's the point," Catherine said the words gently and slowly as if she were speaking to a child.

The girl's hand went to her head once again and slowly came down; there wasn't any blood, just a lump and a sore spot.

She folded her arms and with a roll of her eyes she let out, "Being blind is the point?"

Walking past her toward the fire, Catherine's eyes watched as the flames popped and danced along the wood. "No, it's dark because they come running when they see the light. It's like a bug zapper to them, and I don't have enough bullets to be zapping"."""

The girl never thought about that; she never thought about a lot of things. All she focused on for the past few days was running. She 'spend much time wondering what was chasing her, why they were chasing her, or even how to make them stop. The only thought in her mind was 'keep running'. Long gone were the times when she could sit and plot out her next move or decide how to deal with the monsters next door or down the street. She knew as she stood there in the glow of the fireplace that all that was left was running and surviving.

The young girl nodded as Catherine started to stomp the fire out with her black boots. Turning around slowly, Catherine gave the girl a good once over. She was blonde and thin; her hair hung down her slender back and somewhat rested on the bright red cheeks of her face. She wasn't too tall. From what Catherine could see, they were the same height. She had shorts that were cut too low, and a tight white T-shirt. The sight caused a smile to grow on Catherine's face, and that grew into a small laugh.

"You're just a happy meal on the run, aren't you?" Catherine asked.

The girl leaned back on the fireplace with her arms crossed, turning her head quickly toward Catherine. The girl could make out her smile through the smoke and the moonlight mixture in the room. She put her hands on her hips and said, "What does that mean?"

The caramel-skinned shotgun wielder dropped back in one of the dusty seats with a smile on her face and said, "You're showing a lot of skin, given that you're running from things that love to eat people."

The girl looked down at herself then back over at Catherine. With a roll of her eyes and her best attempt at mocking Catherine she said, "Forgive me for not covering up, Mom! I didn't have much time. Just like you didn't have enough time to clean up for your guest!"

Looking around, Catherine closed her eyes for a moment, partly because she was tired and partly to hide the fact that she was rolling them . Dumb statements were her kryptonite, both in the old world and this new hell they called life. As she let the statement slowly fade from her thoughts, she smiled and said, "This isn't my house, I found it a few days ago, just like you did."

The girl looked around and softly asked, "You got chased here too?"

Catherine sighed and slowly opened up her eyes, "No, I'm looking for someone, two someones really. I'm just holding up here until I get a better idea of what to do, I guess."

The girl nodded as her eyes slowly moved toward the shotgun that was leaning by the staircase. She had one small thought that was growing in her head, getting that shotgun in her hands. She could have darted for the weapon and made a power play for the house, but that thought was shot dead by a picture of Catherine beating what was left of the young girl's life out of her. She stood there staring at the weapon before Catherine's head slowly turned toward the weapon as well.

Catherine smirked and looked back at the girl, "Don't get any ideas," she said.

The girl's head turned toward Catherine and she did her best to flash a smile, "I don't think there are any good ideas left. It comes down to run or fight from what I see."

Catherine leaned forward, letting her fingers dance along her boot laces as if she were tying her shoes. She wasn't worried about taking the girl on in a fair fight, but, if she got to that shotgun, fair would go out the window. Catherine didn't want to gamble her life on who was faster; if the girl moved forward, she would stab, no questions asked. Catherine's heart beat a little faster as her fingers slowly pulled up her pants leg.

The young girl looked down at the floor and softly continued, "I'm too weak to fight, and too slow to run."

Catherine laughed, dropping back in her seat, relieved.

The young girl looked over at Catherine and softly said, "Something funny?"

"I'm sorry. I thought you were making a joke," Catherine said.

The young woman shook her head at the statement. Her whole tone changed as she grimly said, "There's nothing funny about what's going on. There's nothing funny about people dying." She slowly started to take a seat on the floor near the wall, pulling her knees to her chest until they were pressed against her. "There damn sure isn't anything funny about them coming back," she added.

Her blue eyes gazed down at her dirty white shoes. She rubbed one toe over the other trying to dust it off, but the dirt remained. She was trying to avoid continuing their conversation because she wasn't sure if she wanted to open up Pandora's box with the question that was dancing along the tip of her tongue.

There wasn't going to be a happy story, no one had those anymore. Everyone has lost or is looking for someone, but nobody ever finds anyone. That's what the girl was slowly learning these days; this new world was full of loss and no one was coming to terms with that truth. The era of small talk was dead now; everyone was right to the point these days.

The young woman let the words fall from her lips ever so carefully as she asked, "So, umm...who are you looking for?"

Catherine leaned forward in her seat to stare at the young

woman. The bright glow of the moon had made its way through the cracks and gaps in the boarded-up windows. She could make out the outline of the young woman's thin body and even the light-yellow color of her hair. She didn't know the girl and didn't plan on getting to know her. She was a passerby, someone to beat the night with, but not to count on, not to trust. That's what Catherine kept playing in her head.

It was her against the world; no one could be trusted, not anymore, not after last time. "What does it matter?" Catherine smiled and asked.

With a raised eyebrow, the young woman crossed her arms over her chest and said, "You're fucking rude, you know that?"

Catherine laughed and gave the young woman a small nod before leaning back in her seat and continuing.

"What I mean is, you're leaving in the morning, and I might not even be alive next week. I just don't see the point of the conversation."

Catherine rested her head back on the dusty fabric of the chair and stared at the broken ceiling fan that was hovering over them. It was a hopeless thing, hanging on by some old rusty nail. She sighed as her eyes came down from the nails to meet the young girl's blue eyes. "At the end of the day, it doesn't matter." Catherine said.

The girl nodded, slowly uncrossed her arms, and jammed her thumbs back into her small hip pockets. "You don't talk to many people, do you?" the woman asked Catherine.

Catherine laughed. "Not any that were alive, not lately anyways"."

The girl closed her eyes and ran her hands over her face. She kept them there for a moment and let out a loud sigh into her palms before slapping her hands down onto her thighs and softly saying, "I'm just trying to stay alive; I don't really have a plan or anything."

The girl stopped to look down at the blood and dirt that

had stained her white sneakers. She put her thumb down and tried to rub it off as hard as she could, but it wasn't something that she could simply wash away. Just like the monsters outside, all the blood, and all the bodies, were here to stay.

She looked up from her shoes and continued, "I had to leave, there was nothing back there for me. I woke up in the middle of the night and- "

Catherine shot up out of her seat and walked into the darkness of the hallway where the shotgun sat. The girl stopped as her eyes followed Catherine, watching each footstep move as if it were in slow motion. She was sure this was it, that shotgun was coming out for the final time, but then Catherine walked past the rifle, and the young woman sat there staring at it.

When Catherine stepped fully into the darkness, the young woman got to her feet. Her heart beat faster now, she looked around the room, searching for something, anything she could use. Then her eyes found a fire poker resting by the fireplace. Before she knew it, she was standing by the fireplace, her hand was going out toward the poker.

She called out, "Where are you going?"

There was no answer only the sound of cabinets opening and closing. The young woman's heartbeat picked up a faster pace as the thought of the shotgun shells raced through her mind. Her fingers wrapped around the handle of the poker, and she was about to pick it up when she heard Catherine shout back, "You sounded like you're gonna break into a some sob story, and I need a drink or two so I can at least pretend that I care."

The young woman's jaw dropped; she couldn't believe the words that came from the darkness. "I guess all the good people got eaten!" she shouted.

Catherine laughed as she shouted back, "Well, you're still here, so what does that say about you?"

The girl looked down at her fingers that were tightly

wrapped around the fire poker. She didn't break her stare until she heard Catherine's footsteps once again. She dropped the poker back into its rack and waited for Catherine, who returned with a bottle of whiskey and two glasses. Catherine dropped back into her seat, sending dust flying into the air. She placed the glasses on the end table next to the chair and poured the brown liquid into the clear glasses.

The young woman's eyes were fixed on the liquid as it slowly danced along the clear glass, building up a small wave of freedom in the small glass. As much as she wanted to be released from the hell, she was living for just a moment, she could only find herself wishing it was water filling up that glass instead of alcohol. Catherine leaned forward to hand the young woman the glass, but she just stared at Catherine's hand before shaking her head. Leaning on the fireplace, the young girl said, "I don't drink."

Raising her eyebrow, Catherine laughed and asked, "You're kidding me, right? You know the world ended? Now's the best time to become a drinker."

The girl shook her head again, and Catherine leaned back saying, "More for me. So, just when did your world end?"

The girl looked away, and a small smile crawled its way to her lips as she softly said, "Why does it matter?"

Her head turned back toward Catherine, who took a sip of the whiskey and laughed. "Funny," she said before leaning forward, resting her arms on her knees and cupping the glass in both her hands. "When?" Catherine asked once again without looking up from the still brown water that set fire to her empty stomach.

The young girl ran her chipped pink fingernails through her hair before faintly saying, "I guess the same time as everyone else. I heard about it on the news, but for a while, I just thought it was something happening somewhere else, like with the war. It's sad and all, but it's not on your doorstep."

Catherine smiled at the girl's words as she started pulling something from under her tank top. When the sliver chain dropped free of her fingers the young woman could see two metal tags shining in the moonlight,

"My doorstep is a lot closer than yours, sweetheart," Catherine said.

The woman's face turned pink for a short moment before it went full red. She placed her hands over her face and shook her head before dropping them and continuing.

"I didn't mean...what I was trying to say was–" the girl said.

""Catherine laughed and leaned back in her seat once again saying, "Keep the story going, Happy Meal."

The young girl's eyebrow went up then a smile slowly grew on her face, it was a feeling she hadn't felt for a while. Not since she left the complex, not since she left them. She smiled looking down at the floor and then softly said, "My name's Sue."

Catherine took a sip of her drink and then smiled. "Keep the story going, Sue."

Sue nodded and ran her fingers through her hair before starting once again, "I remember thinking that it would never happen in America, like we could stop it somehow. But we didn't know what it was."

Sue paused for a moment as she looked up from her dirty white shoes to Catherine, who was leaning back in the seat and twirling her drink around in her glass. Sue wasn't sure if she was putting on an act, pretending to be jaded by the past. It was something people in this new world liked to do, act as if yesterday was so long ago and today was all that mattered. Sue wasn't sure if she was putting on an act like the rest or if she just wasn't paying attention, but as she stared at her, Sue could see she was miles away in her mind.

Sue leaned on the boarded-up window as she continued,

"Then they were in D.C, then in Atlanta, then, before I knew it, they were down the street."

Catherine nodded as she stared at the brown waves in her glass. "Down the street, up the block, next door..." Catherine downed her glass and placed it on the end table. "And in your house," she added.

Sue nodded. She folded her arms over her chest, looked at Catherine and said, "I woke up to some loud banging in the middle of the night. I remember looking outside my window, I could see them pushing their way into the house. There was moaning. No words, just moaning. I remember hearing my friends shouting. I remember seeing their blood." A small tear pushed its way out of Sue's left eye; her hand went up to meet it, but, before she could whip it away, it was accompanied by a stream of new tears. "Oh God," she softly said.

Catherine wanted to tell her it was okay; she wanted to say that everything was going to be fine. But she knew that was a lie. She knew whatever horror story Sue was replaying in her head would be stuck on replay for the rest of her life. It wouldn't fade away; it was just going to get longer and bloodier as time went by.

"They broke through the front door. There must have been 20 of them. Just knocking over things, moaning, and smelling like, like," Sue closed her eyes hoping to lock the word away and never be forced to say it, ever.

Catherine knew the smell all too well. She leaned forward and softly spoke, as if to whisper to herself, "Death."

Sue cleared her tears away again as she nodded and continued, "Yeah, my friends Samantha and Dean, they–" Sue paused once more as her eyes dropped down to the floor.

Catherine shook her head and stood up. "I'm sorry about that. You got any family?"

Sue shook her head at the question. She had a mother in Alabama, but it wasn't a relationship worth crossing a zombie-covered state for. She merely assumed her mother was eaten by the zombies or died years ago from alcohol poisoning.

"Do you have a car?" Catherine asked.

Sue was pulled back into the real world by that question. She brushed the rest of the tears from her face as she shook her head once again. "It ran out of gas about two or three miles down the road," Sue said, causing Catharine to roll her eyes and drop back into her seat, knocking over the glass on the end table.

"Shit! Can I not get a fucking break? Jesus."

A weak laugh filled the empty room and then it grew, Catherine's eyes found Sue. The young girl put her hand up and fought to stop laughing.

"That's what I said word for word when it stopped moving," Sue said.

Catherine shook her head, but, before she knew it, she was laughing along. It was odd; neither of them really knew what they were laughing about. The fact that they were fighting their way through a world of zombies on foot really wasn't a laughing matter, but there they were laughing. Until Sue began crying once again.

Catherine grabbed the second empty glass and filled it up with the whiskey. Sue quickly got to her feet, and through the haze her tears created, she could see the brown waves of the glass coming closer. She stared at it and then said, "I told you I don't drink."

Catherine nodded and grabbed Sue's hand, placing the glass in it. "You do now. All that crying is gonna get you killed or get you to kill yourself."

Catherine turned back around and walked to the staircase. She leaned over before her foot hit the bottom step and picked up the shotgun. "Drink up, you'll sleep better," Catherine said as she started to walk up the steps.

"Wait!" Sue called out into the darkness. Catherine turned

around to see the young woman standing in the doorway. "When did your world go to hell?"

Catherine looked at the outline of Sue in the doorway and sighed as she rested her shotgun over her shoulder. "You're really not gonna let it go, huh? What does it matter?"

Sue groaned at the question, and Catherine could see her shadowy figure storming back into the moonlight of the living room. "Whatever," Sue said as she turned her back on the subject. Sue only got two steps before she heard Catherine's words fill up the dimly lit room.

"I didn't make it home for dinner."

Sue's head turned back toward the staircase. Catherine stood at the top; her eyes were fixed on Sue, but her mind was fading back to that fateful day as the words left her lips.

"All that craziness was going on, and I told them I'd be home. I told them to lock up because mommy was coming home for dinner."

Catherine's body slowly crumbled down onto the staircase. She sat there with the shotgun resting on her lap. Catherine's eyes went up from the black barrel to Sue, who was standing at the bottom of the steps staring at her.

"The highway was packed as shit. There were fires, overturned cars, and those freaks running about everywhere. There were tons of them, just making their way down the highway as if they owned the city. I did my best to drive through them, to just keep pushing home, but they started to pile on the car," Catherine added.

Sue leaned on the railing and shook her head as she said, "I would have been scared out my mind."

Catherine looked down at her and softly said, "I still am. Someone told me they smell fear; that's how they know where you are." Catherine smiled for a moment as her fingers ran along the metal barrel of the shotgun. "I guess they'll always know where I am."

Catherine stopped for a moment, staring down at the black, cool metal of the shotgun, trying to fight back tears. Sue understood that feeling too well. She went to move closer, in some sad attempt to comfort her. Yet, when her foot hit the step, Catherine's head shot up to stare at her. The two women locked eyes for what felt like forever, both of them hiding rivers of tears behind their gaze. Catherine slowly moved the shotgun from off her lap and stood it up on the buttstock.

She held onto the barrel and rested her head on it slightly as she softly said, "I called my husband; I told him I loved him, that I would always love him and to kiss Jordan for me. I couldn't go forward, so I backed the car up as far as I could."

The tone in Catherine's voice caused Sue to slowly sit down on the bottom step. She rested her back on the railing and stared up at Catherine, lost in the words she was hearing, lost in the emotion of it all. Catherine sighed as Sue gently asked, "What did you do?"

"I slammed on the gas, running the car and those dead fucking hitchhikers right off into the river." Catherine barked a laugh.

Sue smiled and said, "Bullshit!"

Catherine shook her head. "It was the only thing I could think of"."

Sue's eyes went wide. "Well damn! I could have thought of a million other things," Sue said with a smile, then turned her head to the side, looking back into the moonlight of the living room before adding, "But then again, most of those things would have gotten me killed." She grinned.

"Or send you running through the woods in the middle of the night"," Catherine chimed in.

Sue laughed and nodded. "Very true. So, then what happened?" she asked.

"They can't swim all that well. I found that out, so I waited until a couple of them followed me in, and I took off toward land. I started my way on foot to the house. I had to lose the heels because it was a few miles down the way. I'm still broken up about that," she said with a small smile.

She shook her head as she got back to her feet saying, "Anyway, mommy was late for dinner. I got there and the door was open. The lights were on, but no one was home."

Catherine started back up the stairs as Sue asked into the darkness, "Are they...?"

Catherine turned around and shook her head ."No, my boys are too smart to end up on some zombie's menu. They're somewhere; I just need to find them. I helped myself to a car and headed south toward Savannah. My mother-in-law lives there, so I'm guessing that's where they're at."

Sue nodded at Catherine's words and looked back down at the floor and asked quietly, "Savannah?"

Catherine nodded and said, "Yeah, I ran into some people at a Walmart, loaded up with some things. Nothing too crazy, water, guns, knives, a shit load of tuna." Catherine laughed and shook her head. "Jordan hates tuna."

Sue nodded at her words, not turning to face the woman as she continued once again.

"They said they would help me get to Savannah, but when I woke up, they were gone; they'd taken my car and my supplies. They left me there to die. I took what I could carry on my back and hoped I'd run into another car. Never did. I saw a few drive pass, but they didn't stop. I can't say I blame them."

Sue's head finally turned toward Catherine. Her eyes filled with tears, and she rushed to clear them away. She didn't want to explain them; she just hoped the darkness of the room hid them from Catherine's view. Sue stood up on the bottom step and pushed to put on a smile and hoped her voice didn't give away the pain and confusion she held inside. "Well, we can use my car, it's only a few miles down the road."

Catherine put the shotgun on her shoulder as she added, "And out of gas."

Sue closed her eyes and sighed as she remembered the large fact that caused her to run through the woods in the first place. "Right"."

She stared down at the ground for a moment then looked back up with a small smile once again. "There was a sign down the road for a gas station. We can go there. Get some gas and then hit the road."

Peering into the darkness, Catherine rolled her eyes and started walking down toward Sue. She said, "I passed that place, and there are tons of those zombies running around. Besides, I'm going to Savannah. Alone."

Sue nodded, trying to keep up her weak smile as she stepped up to meet Catherine. The two women were just two steps away from each other now.

"Yeah, I know, but we're safer together. You don't know what Savannah's like right now. You might need help. I can go with you and- " Sue jumped a little as her words were cut off by Catherine's laughter coming from the darkness.

Catherine took another step down and leaned forward, looking Sue in her light blue eyes as she said, "I've heard this before. I walked for days before I found this place because someone wanted to help." She stood leering at Sue with the shotgun held tightly in her right hand. She put it up between the two of them for a moment before letting the pump handle of the shotgun fall into her left hand. "Story time's over."

Catherine turned back around and started back up the steps. She was halfway up when she noticed Sue's footsteps following her. She spun around and said,

"You got the memory of a fucking goldfish or something? You didn't hear me the first time? You stay down here!"

Catherine glared at Sue; she was waiting for the girl to back her way down the steps, but instead she stood there with her arms over her chest.

"So, what's your plan? To just sit here, get drunk and crawl your way to Savannah?" Sue asked as she ran her fingers through her blonde hair. "Like it or not, I can help you and you can help me. We need each other."

Catherine pulled back the pump handle of the shotgun, and the loud metallic sound of a round being loaded filled the house. Sue was sweating, not from the Georgia summer night, but from the force of her heart pounding in her chest. She put her hands up and started slowly walking back down the steps. With a smile, Catherine said, "If you hear a moan, just scream."

Sue stood there at the bottom of the steps watching as Catherine walked up the steps and finally out of her view. Sue heard a door slam, and she dropped her arms.

"What a bitch, no wonder no one's looking for you," she said quietly into the darkness.

Sue started back over toward the fireplace; she sat down in the dusty old chair and glanced over at the whiskey bottle and the glass she had left on the table. She didn't want to tell or hear any more stories about dead people. All she wanted to do was stay alive, and the crazy woman upstairs was her best bet at that. Sue pulled her legs into the seat and grabbed the glass of whiskey. She stared at it for a moment and then downed it like a shot. She shook her head and stuck out her tongue before she finally rested her head on the arm of the chair and closed her eyes.

She couldn't stop herself from thinking about the woman's story, and how she was so strong, brave, and dead inside. She treated kindness as if it were a weakness. Sue tossed and turned as she thought about the woman's husband, Jordan, and Savannah. They were the little bit of hope that woman was holding onto, and it didn't seem fair to take that away from her. It didn't seem right to tell her Savannah was lost. That was the part of the story conveniently left out. She needed the woman strong, not broken and hopeless.

Before Sue knew it, she was fast asleep. She was dreaming of better days, partying with her friends, drinking, and having fun like any other college student. Then the lights went out, and the dream turned dark. She was running from another one of those zombies. She could smell him right behind her as she raced through the woods, just like before. But this time there was no house, no crazy woman to save her. This time Sue fell.

When she rolled over, she felt the zombie grab her by the arms. He shook her back and forth. She felt him tearing into her skin. Then as he leaned in with his bloody jagged teeth aimed for her neck, Sue's eyes shot open and she screamed.

It was daytime, and Catherine was standing over her.

2
___

THIS IS NO SUNDAY SCHOOL PICNIC

PLANET DEAD

"*Wake the hell up!*" Catherine shouted into Sue's face.

Sue sat there, her shirt full of sweat, and her skin pale white. Catherine rolled her eyes and took her hands off of Sue's shoulders. She had been shaking the girl awake for some time now, in hopes of stopping her screaming.

"You were talking in your sleep the whole damn night," Catherine said.

Sue's heart was racing; sweat rushed down her neck as she looked around the room.

"I thought..." Sue softly said, not sure where to go with the statement.

Catherine nodded. "I know what you thought, but it was just a nightmare."

Sue got up slowly followed Catherine, who had taken off toward the kitchen. She watched as Catherine pulled out some bottled waters and Pop-Tarts from a black bag on the kitchen table. With the sun breaking its way through the cracks of the boarded-up windows, it was easier for Sue to see how far gone the house was. She had thought at first that the boards were placed there to keep the zombies out, but after looking at the rusted sink and the broken cabinet doors, she knew the house had been long forgotten before the zombies arrived.

"The breakfast of champions, you want some?" Catherine asked, and Sue shook her head.

Catherine sighed and said," You've got to eat something, or you won't make it out there."

She tossed the box of tarts at Sue and placed two water bottles in the middle of the table.

Sue held the tarts in her hands, staring at them before softly letting out, "So you're not coming then?"

Catherine pulled up a seat and took a bite of her frosted treat. She closed her eyes, trying to avoid Sue's gaze.

Sue nodded. "I see. I didn't want to say anything last night, but there is nothing left in Savannah. Nothing alive anyways."

The words came out cold, and Sue wished they didn't. She wished she didn't say anything at all. But the thought of her going back into that world alone angered her. If Sue was truly honest, it scared her.

Catherine looked over at Sue, her eyes locked on the young girl. "That's where I went to school, that's where I just came from. I know."

Catherine slowly started to get to her feet and said, "You woke up in the middle of the night to an attack. How do you know if there is anything left? You woke up and you ran." Catherine walked over to Sue and smiled. "You were wrong, Sue, running seems like the only thing you know how to do. So why don't you just keep doing it and get the hell out of here."

Sue looked down as Catherine walked past her.

"Stupid!" Sue said she slapped her hand into her forehead and sighed. She knew that reaction was going to come, but she let her emotions win. Savannah was lost, but that wasn't a conversation they needed to have, not if they were going to stay together, which was all Sue wanted.

"Look, I'm sorry, but I'm not going to make it out there alone. I don't have a gun, I don't have–"

Sue was cut off quickly as Catherine turned around with a laugh. "I don't give a damn."

Sue screamed back, "Fuck you! You think you can just give me some water and a box of old Pop-Tarts and say have a nice day!"

Catherine nodded and moved forward as she pulled out a handgun and pointed it at Sue. Sue stood there looking down the barrel of the gun. She didn't start crying, she didn't put her hands up or try to avoid the shot, she just stared. Looking past the barrel into Catherine's eyes, Sue said, "This is getting old."

Catherine pulled back the hammer and Sue dropped the box of pop-tarts. With a smile, Catherine released the hammer and turned the gun around, handle first, toward Sue.

"You got six bullets in there. Rule number one is always save one for yourself."

Sue looked at the gun and then quickly took it as she nodded and said, "Thanks."

Sue got down and picked up the box and then grabbed a water bottle off the table. She placed them in a small shopping bag, then started toward the front door. She pushed the gun into the back of her pants and slowly wrapped her fingers around the doorknob.

"I'm sorry," Sue said, and paused for a moment to look into Catherine's eyes. Sue saw all the pain that Catherine tried to hide behind her light brown eyes, and Sue softly continued with, "I do hope you find your family."

Catherine nodded as she said, "I hope you live."

Sue pulled open the door. The bright light took over her view, and her hand shot up to block it. Her surroundings looked nothing like it did the night before. The dead bodies were still lying a few feet away from the front door.

This Is No Sunday School Picnic

Sue turned around and looked at Catherine as she asked, "What's your name anyway?"

Catherine smiled and walked toward Sue as she said, "What does it matter?"

Sue shook her head and walked down the front steps .

"You're crazy, you know that?" Sue replied as Catherine watched her walk off into the tall grass and into the woods from which she came.

Sue kept her head forward and fought not to look back. She had so much fear building up inside of her, but she knew she had to overcome it because she was on her own now. She wasn't sure what to do; she could head down the road a little more, get some gas, and then double back to the car, but she had an odd feeling she wouldn't make it back from that trip. She kept walking through the shade of the woods until she dropped her bag and ran her fingers through her hair.

She fought back tears as she whispered, "What the hell am I doing?"

The question was a loaded one, she didn't have a plan. There was no step two in her formula of survival and even if there were, she ran through the woods in the middle of the night, she didn't know what path would take her back to the road. She heard small footsteps coming up behind her, which caused Sue to smile.

"I knew you weren't as mean as you were letting on." Sue turned around slowly and laughed. "Thank you, because I'm—"

Her words stopped as her eyes rested on who was behind her. Sue was face to face with a large, bloody bald man. Bloody white jawbone was showing through a hole in his cheek. A bloody bit of flesh was hanging from the hole. She could see the man's blood-red set of teeth.

Sue screamed as her hand raced toward her back for the gun. Yet, the man's arms were faster. He grabbed hold of Sue.

The gun fell to the ground.

Sue was pushing and punching; her skin was turning red from the blood and the force of her body fighting to get off the ground.

Her elbow broke free and slammed into the bloody man's jaw. He fell over to the side. Sue shot up and started running through the woods once again. The dead man was moving quickly behind her. She tripped. Slamming into the ground, Sue let out a gust of air. The wind had been knocked out of her, so she just stayed there. Unmoved by the madness that was behind her.

When the man let out a moan, Sue slowly rolled over, looking up at the monster that was there to take her life. The zombie grabbed hold of her arms once again, but now he was sitting down on her, pinning her to the ground. He smelled of rotting meat as he leaned in closer to Sue, his jaw opening wide.

Sue screamed, then heard a loud blast; warm blood was quick to cover her body.. Sue fell to the ground with the zombie's lifeless body on top of her. She pushed and fought once again to get out from under it. When she was finally free, Sue looked up to see the woman from the house pointing a shotgun in her face.

Catherine was smiling as she hovered over Sue with her shotgun. She lowered the barrel and said, "I'm Catherine Briggs, and you better hope none of that blood got in your mouth."

3

I THINK YOU JUST COMPLAIN JUST TO HEAR YOURSELF TALK

PLANET DEAD

"Wait up!" Sue said as she bent over, panting while a river of sweat ran down her back. She looked up to see Catherine soldiering through the heat with most of their gear on her back. "I said hold up!" Sue shouted. Her hair was still stained a dark red from the blood that covered her only hours before. Sue longed for a hot shower, but those days of bubble baths and hot meals felt like misguided daydreams now. That stage of life was over.

In less than three months, the United States had fallen into an undead circle of hell with the rest of the world. The dead outnumbered the living, and humanity as a whole was over. Death was all that remained.

"Wait up, Briggs! You act like we have a deadline or something," Sue said.

Catherine stopped and turned around slowly, she stood still as she watched Sue struggling her way down the black road.

"All you do is complain. I should have let that guy eat your little ass back there." Catherine placed her hands on the top of her head looking up at the clear blue skies. She closed her eyes and hoped, damn near prayed, for just one slight breeze. Yet, as she opened her eyes and felt the sting of sweat making its way past her eyelashes, she knew there was no saving grace to come. "And don't call me Briggs. Uncle Sam's dead and the war's over."

Catherine took in the sight of Sue's dirty white shoes awkwardly slapping into the black top as Sue ran up next to her. The girl was young, skinny, blonde, and severely out of shape. Catherine had to look back every few steps just to make sure Sue was still alive. Catherine's hands dropped from her head. "You're not gonna make it," Catherine said very matter-of-factly.

Sue was once again leaning over, gazing at the sweat that dropped between her dirty white sneakers as she attempted to catch her breath. Sue's head slowly came up as Catherine started to speak once again in that tone, that tone of truth and petty mixed into one, much like a teacher's tone as they listed all the reasons why you failed the semester.

"Life is like a fucked-up horror movie now," Catherine said.

Sue cleared the sweat from her brows. Hanging over staring at the asphalt, Sue fought to catch her breath and said, "What?"

Catherine patted Sue's back. "Being young, pretty, and popular isn't enough," Catherine said. Pulling out their last bottle of water, Catherine opened it and handed it to Sue. "You gotta fight if you wanna make it out alive, and by the looks of it, you're not a fighter," Catherine said with a laugh.

Sue put the clear liquid heaven to her lips and closed her eyes. A lukewarm rush of relief made its way past her lips and danced along her tongue before both air and water rushed their way down her throat When Sue opened her eyes, the water bottle was an empty, sunken shell. Sue's hands ran down her sweaty thighs trying to ease the itch the repetitive movement started to create. Sue looked up at Catherine, and their eyes locked for a small moment before Sue tossed the bottle at Catherine's feet.

"Go fuck yourself." Sue pushed past Catherine and continued down the road yelling, "Had I known the world was going to be taken over by zombies, I would have spent a little more time in the gym." Sue put her hand over her eyes to block out the sun as she turned to look back at Catherine and asked, "How much longer 'til we get there?"

Catherine laughed and casually strolled over to Sue. She knew women like her from the Army. Barbie dolls who weren't worth a damn in a firefight. Soldiers you couldn't count on for a glass of water, much less having your back. Yet, one thing Catherine learned from her years in the Army was that in every toy box full of Barbies, there was always one that doubled as the G.I Jane edition. She just had to break her heels before she could put on her boots. Catherine wasn't sure if that was Sue or not, but she hoped that was the case because the alternative was too dark to think about.

"We'll be there soon enough," Catherine said.

Catherine's tan combat boots slowed to match the pace of Sue's dirty white sneakers as the two women made their way along the dead road toward their gas station of hope. Catherine ran her hand along the back of her neck, clearing away a river of sweat that ran down her hot skin. She could feel the handle of the shotgun brush against her knuckles. She thought for a moment how there was no sweeter feeling than the cold metal of a shotgun. Then the thought of Robert popped into her head, his big arms wrapping around her as he whispered, *'it's gonna be okay.'* There was something far sweeter than a shotgun. She just needed to get to it.

"It's crazy, isn't it?" Sue's words pulled Catherine out of her heartbreaking moment. Her hand went up to clear a tear from her eye, one that she was ready to call sweat if asked about it. Catherine's head turned toward Sue, who was walking with her hands on her head.

"What's crazy?" Catherine asked.

Sue's eyes scanned along the long road ahead. She told herself she was scanning the area, that she was being Catherine's eyes in hopes of removing the feeling of being a burden from her mind. "All of this. I mean, fucking zombies? Of all the things I thought would happen, seeing the dead come to life wasn't one of them," Sue said.

Catherine nodded, but she wasn't fully listening. Her mind was on the heat and the lack of food they had. One of them would be passing out soon, and Catherine hoped it wasn't her. The thought of Sue being their only line of defense scared the shit out of her.

"I heard that this all happened because of some drunk driver," Sue said as she looked over at Catherine. "It was some truck driver over in Russia."

Hanging her thumbs through her belt loops and resting her hands along her side, she looked around and continued her story. "Dean saw an article about it. The driver was carrying a large shipment of toxic waste."

Catherine stopped walking and put her hand up. "Wait a minute, where did you say you heard all this again?" she asked.

Sue kept walking and didn't even look back at Catherine as she said, "It was all over the Internet."

Catherine rolled her eyes and started walking slowly alongside Sue once again. "You know that's bullshit, right?" Catherine said.

Sue shrugged and said, "Dean said the government covered it up, and with who we put in office..."

Catherine shook her head and laughed. "Shut up!"

Sue rolled her eyes. "That's what happened."

Catherine ran her hand over her face and cleared away the sweat. She sighed and then started laughing as she walked and said, "Sounds like you and Dean watched too many comic book movies."

Sue laughed and nodded. "Well, Dean did have a pretty big comic book collection."

Catherine's full lips formed into a large grin, and through the smile she asked, "So, you and Dean were, you know?" Catherine winked and elbowed Sue.

Sue laughed shaking her head "No, we didn't even know each other before all this. I mean he was in some of my classes, but we didn't hang around the same people."

Catherine nodded and pulled at a strap, adjusting her backpack. "So, you three just ended up together in some house?"

Sue nodded as she squinted her eyes to look over at Catherine. "It was my sorority house. Well, the new one because we got kicked off campus."

Catherine quickly let out, "I knew it!"

Sue stopped walking. "Knew what?"

Catherine scanned the area and pointed. "It's up ahead."

Sue folded her arms and stood her ground as she watched Catherine. "You knew what?"

Catherine rolled her eyes at Sue and said, "That you were one of those Alpha Alpha Alpha party girls. You know, Jell-O shots and bad decisions."

Sue began walking down the street again, her pace much faster than before. She pushed past Catherine.

Catherine laughed and wagged her finger at Sue. "You're gonna stop pushing me like that before I start pushing back, little girl."

Sue turned around, throwing her arms in the air. "You don't even know me! You don't know shit about me!"

Catherine rushed toward the girl. Her hand slapped over Sue's lips, holding her mouth shut.

"I know you need to keep your damn mouth shut," Catherine whispered.

She held Sue still, looking over the blonde girl's shoulder to see the figures moving around by the gas station. Catherine pushed Sue back and removed the backpack she was carrying, dropping it to the ground.

"They're waking up," Catherine said.

Sue looked over at the gas station that was just a few feet down the road. She put her hand up to block out the sun as she watched the figures under the awning slowly start to come alive. Her hand dropped.

"I didn't think they slept," Sue said.

Catherine said, "They don't, they just get real still when there isn't anything to chase." She pushed her shotgun to the side and tossed her leather jacket to the ground as she pulled something out that reflected the sunlight into Sue's eyes.

Sue's head turned away from the light, and she could see more zombies making their way out of the gas station.

"Oh fuck," Sue said, pointing at the gas station. "We got more of them."

Catherine walked past her with a shiny metal machete in her hand.

"Really? You think? Grab the bag!" Catherine said as her tan boots made a beeline for the gas station.

Sue sprinted back to the bag and zipped it up as she swung it over her shoulder and ran behind Catherine. Sue's footsteps came to an abrupt stop as Catherine stood still, staring at the hoard of zombies that were one by one turning to face them. Sue dropped the bag and pulled out her gun.

Catherine shook her head. "No guns."

Sue's eyebrow raised. "You're kidding, right?"

Catherine shook her head again, and her fingers tightened around the handle of her machete. "We're running low on bullets."

Sue laughed and lowered her gun. "Bullets aren't gonna do us any good if we're dead."

Sue's words caused Catherine to look over her shoulder at the girl. Nodding at her, Catherine took one deep breath before she took off running toward the mass of zombies that were forming. Sue looked down at the gun in her hand and then up at the path that Catherine had blazed.

"You can do this. You can do this." Sue closed her eyes and whispered to herself again, "You can do this."

When she opened her eyes, Sue saw Catherine's arm swing savagely toward one of the oncoming zombies Before Sue could blink again, she saw the zombie's severed head flying through the air, casting a stream of dark blood through the blue sky and onto the black asphalt.

Sue shook her head and shouted, "I can't do this!"

Catherine was too deep in the bloodshed to hear the cry of self-doubt coming from Sue's lips. A tan boot went lunging into the chest of a large black man in bloodstained gray overalls. The man fell backwards, toppling over a trash can as he crashed into the ground. The man, or what was left of the man, fought to get to his feet before Catherine's blade sliced into the middle of his head.

The blade was sharp enough to slice through the body, but Catherine had to tug hard to rip it from the man's skull. Catherine turned around, swinging her machete into the neck of another nearby zombie, when her eyes went back to the road.

"Sue!" Catherine screamed out, but the only reply she received was the low hungry moans of the zombies that were quickly surrounding her. She spun the machete around in her hand, her eyes hopped from left to right.

From female zombie to male...

From young zombie to old.

Catherine's blade flew forward and connected with an old woman's head. The blade drove deep into the skull, causing Catherine to drag the old woman's head and body to the ground as she attempted to yank the weapon free. Just as she felt the blade start to wiggle loose, a pair of arms wrapped around her. Catherine's hands released the handle of the machete. Her elbow went flying back into the ribs of the dead, but as she connected, she felt her elbow cave into the body cavity of the zombie.

Catherine's arm came back covered in blood and black, rancid-smelling tissue. Yet, even with his organs falling down onto Catherine's tan boots, the man wouldn't release her. Catherine leaned back and then swung forward, pushing her hips back as she sent the zombie hurling toward the ground in front of her. Catherine had no time to bask in her beautiful escape. There were a handful of zombies left; more than she wanted to deal with. She tightened her jaw as she thought about how she allowed herself to fall into a mess like this again. Catherine trusted another person, and just like the last, she was left high and dry. Her fist went up slowly, and a small bit of guts fell from her elbow to the ground.

"Bring it on, motherfuckers!" When the words left her lips, she heard a loud blast and saw the kneecap of a nearby zombie explode, sending blood splattering along the concrete.

The zombie did its best to maneuver toward his would-be dinner, but he quickly fell over as his hands swung and slashed at the air. Once he was out of the way, Catherine could see clearly what had stepped in to pull her from the jaws of death, better yet, whom. She could see Sue slowly getting up from the ground, rubbing her lower back.

"Son of a bitch!" Sue said as she leaned over to pick the shotgun up off the ground. She rested the butt on her midsection, and she turned to aim at another zombie. Sue's finger tightened around the cool metal trigger; she closed her eyes as she pulled back and heard a loud click. Sue's eyes opened, and she turned the shotgun upside down looking into the barrel.

"What happened?" she said softly.

Looking up, Sue saw Catherine racing toward her, machete in hand and screaming, "Reload it!"

Sue's head spun from left to right looking for the large backpack. She ripped open the pockets, glancing up to see Catherine going to war with what was left of the zombie hoard. Flashes of metal and splashes of blood cut through the hot summer air. Sue's eyes connected with one zombie whose attention had quickly moved from Catherine onto Sue. Sue's head dropped back to the backpack as her hand trembled, pulling out the box of red shells.

Sue lifted the lid and then jumped as Catherine screamed out, "Motherfucker!" The bullets leaped from the box and scattered across the ground.

"No. No! No!" Sue said repeatedly as she crawled across the ground, trying to get two of the red shells. Her hand grabbed ahold of the two red cylinders. She rolled over on her back and fumbled with the shotgun, pulling at every bit of metal that would move. "Come on!" Sue screamed. Her eyes went up to see a pair of grey eyes staring down at her.

Sue's eyes immediately watered as the rancid scent of the woman filled the air. The tears blurred the image of the zombie as its mouth opened wide, showing its bloodstained teeth. That feeling of dread and death washed over Sue once again as the zombie let out an ear-splitting scream. Sue closed her eyes. She was sure she would feel the pain of torn skin and the rush of warm blood cover her, but all she felt were warm droplets, like a summer rainfall.

When Sue opened her eyes, she saw the tip of a large blade pushing through the open mouth of the zombie. Sue's eyes went wide, and her hands finally clicked the shotgun into place as Catherine pulled her machete up and through the skull of the female zombie.

The zombie collapsed to the ground, and Catherine smiled. "What's that now, three times I've had to save your-"

Catherine's words were cut off as Sue swung the barrel of the shotgun up at Catherine and pulled back on the trigger.

Catherine dropped down to the ground with her hands over her ears trying her best to block out the effects of the blast. Her ears were ringing, and she could see Sue lying back on the ground once again with the shotgun to her side. As Catherine started to raise, a large body dropped down by her feet. Where once there was a head now only a stump shooting out dark blood all over a blue handicap parking space remained.

Catherine looked at the body then looked over at Sue and laughed, "Well, look at you!"

Sue put her hand over her face. "I'm just gonna lay here for a little bit."

Catherine cupped her hand to her ear and screamed, "What!"

Sue sighed into her hands and sat up looking at Catherine, who was snapping her fingers along her left ear.

"I'm not like that," Sue said, and Catherine's eyes slowly made their way toward Sue.

Catherine walked over, dusted off a section of the ground next to Sue and sat down with her blood-soaked jeans. She rested the machete between her legs and took in the view of dead bodies that lined the gas station.

"Like what?" Catherine asked.

Sue looked over at Catherine and said, "I'm in recovery...""
She laughed and looked at the puddle of blood that was quickly surrounding her sneakers. ""Or I was."

She looked over to Catherine. "What's the worst thing you've ever done?"

Catherine looked over at the blonde girl with the sprinkles of blood that covered her face, and then looked away. "When I first got out of the military, I got a job with this law firm." Catherine rubbed her thumb over the black handle of the machete and closed her eyes. "There was this little girl. I can't remember her name, but she came in with her aunt. They wanted me to represent the little girl in court. She was a cutie or would have been if she ever smiled." Catherine opened her eyes to look back at the bloodshed that covered the ground. "They said the girl's daddy had been doing things to her, some very un-fatherly things." She looked over at Sue.

Sue shook her head. "That's sick."

Catherine nodded and softly said, "Yeah." Catherine got to her feet and rolled her shoulders as she continued, "The little girl shot her parents while they were sleeping one night. They wanted to plead self-defense due to the abuse, and I was geared up and ready for it. I wanted that case so bad."

Sue looked up at Catherine. "What happened?"

Catherine looked down at Sue. "My firm said there wasn't enough proof to back the girl's story, and they didn't want to risk taking on a losing case." She looked down at the ground and shook her head. "I had to tell that little girl that, after all she had been through, I couldn't help her. She cried and screamed, 'Please, Mrs. Briggs, please,' but there wasn't anything I could do." Catherine's fingers tightened around the handle of the machete and she softly said, "That's the worst thing I've ever done."

Sue sat there staring up at Catherine. She stood up and ran her bloodstained hands down her shorts.

"I let my friend drive us home from a party. I was drunk, but she was worse, and I should have called someone, or just told her no, but I just laughed and nodded, thinking everything would be fine." Sue started walking toward the shop doors of the gas station. "We hit a tree just three miles from home. I woke up in the hospital with a broken collarbone, but she didn't make it." Looking over her shoulder at Catherine, Sue said, "I don't drink, haven't for two years now." She pulled open the shop doors. "I'll turn the pumps on and grab some food."

Sue came out a few minutes later with a bag of water and another bag of junk food. "This place didn't have much, but we can double back with the van- " Sue stopped as she saw

Catherine staring at the road. She walked up next to Catherine and looked at her. "What's up?"

Catherine pointed and said, "Something's coming."

Sue stared down the road as a white van rapidly sped into view. "Maybe they can give us a ride to my van, then we can gas it up and- "

Catherine bolted back toward the gas station. Sue stood for a moment before quickly following behind her. Catherine got on the ground, picking up the loose shotgun shells.

"What are you doing?" Sue asked.

Catherine didn't even look up at Sue; she just continued to toss things into the bag. "The fuck you think I'm doing? Getting our shit together and getting out of here."

Sue looked over at the road once again and then back at Catherine. "I know you haven't talked to a lot of people, but don't you think you're overreacting?"

Catherine looked up at Sue, but, before she could answer and tell her how stupid she sounded, the van came to a stop.

Catherine slowly got up from her knees and stood side by side with Sue as the driver of the van let down his window. Old country music blasted from inside the van as a young man in a black baseball cap poked his head out with a smile.

"Y'all got any gas?" the young man asked.

Sue's eyes widened as she got a full view of the guy. She smiled and whispered, "He's cute."

Catherine turned around slowly toward the shotgun lying on the ground as she whispered back, "Well, cutie pie is about to get a mouthful of shotgun."

Catherine's hand crept toward the handle of the shotgun, but Sue grabbed it. "You can't go around shooting people," Sue whispered as the man took in the bloodbath that was once the gas station parking lot.

"Goddamn, did y'all do this?" the man said.

Sue pointed her finger at Catherine. "No, Kill Bill over here did all this," she said and turned on her heels toward the van. "It's gonna be okay," she said to Catherine.

Catherine stood still and closed her eyes as she listened to Sue walking to the van. She whispered to herself, "I should have shot your ass."

Sue smiled as she placed her hands on the lowered window of the van, her fingertips resting along the cold glass. "Sweet baby Jesus, he has AC!" Sue said.

The guy laughed and rolled down the rest of his window slowly, watching Sue's fingers follow the glass. "That I do, y'all need a lift somewhere?" he asked.

Sue nodded, and Catherine sighed as she turned and walked to the van.

"We're good." Catherine said.

Sue rolled her eyes. "Sorry, my friend was raised by wolves. We're trying to make it back to the highway."

"Well, if you girls want, I can take y'all to the highway. It's no problem," the man said with a smile, leaning out the window closer to Sue. "It's up to you."

Sue smiled, turning to look at Catherine, who shook her head and said, "Your mother never told you not to get in the van with the creepy guy who's giving out candy?" Sue's eyebrows went up, and Catherine rolled her eyes and pointed at the van. "Creepy van." She looked over at the driver and pointed. "Candyman!"

The young man stared at Catherine and said, "You know I can hear you, right?"

Catherine looked over at him. "No offense."

The man put his hand up and smiled. "None taken. Listen, I'm heading south. If you want, I can take you to the highway, and you never have to see me again."

Sue kept her eyes on Catherine "You wanna see your family, right?" Catherine bit down on her lip and slowly started walking toward the van, Sue put her hand on

Catherine's shoulder and said, "It's gonna be okay. Come on."

Sue slid open the van door, and Catherine turned around.

"Let me just get our- "

"Catherine!" Sue screamed.

Before Catherine could turn back around, she felt a blow to the back of her head, and she smacked into the ground.

~

"*M*ommy? Mommy?" Catherine turned her head slowly. She could feel a sharp pain pulsating from the back of her head to the front.

"Jordan?" She let the name come out weakly and softly.

"Mommy? You got to wake up; you got to wake up." Catherine's eyes shot open only to see the tan darkness of a sack over her head. There was a metal taste in Catherine's mouth. She rolled her tongue around until she felt the sting of her busted lip. She wanted to kill Sue.

After she broke them free and got back on the right path to finding her family, Catherine was sure she was going to kill Sue, or at the very least, break a bone or two.

She could make out a small bit of light from the moon pushing through the mesh of the tan sack. Hanging by her arms, Catherine slowly swung back and forth in the cool night air. She turned her head to the left and then the right as she whispered, "Sue?"

It was a few moments before Sue said softly, "Catherine?"

Catherine closed her eyes as Sue spoke again, "Don't worry everything's going to be- "

Catherine screamed, "If you say everything's gonna be okay one more fucking time, I swear I'll rip what's left of your brain out!"

They hung by their ropes, slowly swinging in the night air,

taking in the stomach-turning scent of the room. It was a mix of rotten meat and shit. It was so strong it filled Catherine's mouth, so much so she could taste it. She dropped her head down and closed her eyes.

"Mama's coming," she said softly to herself. She rolled her ankle slowly. "Mama's coming!"

4

DYING TOGETHER ISN'T GOING TO SOLVE ANYTHING

PLANET DEAD

*S*winging back and forth in that still summer night, Catherine and Sue resembled old southern wind chimes, each equipped with their own unique sounds that seemed to echo through the night.

"I'm sorry," Sue would say.

"Drop dead," Catherine would fiercely reply.

A muffled sigh was heard from under Sue's dirty tan sack. Sue softly let out words that she was fighting to believe herself: "This could have happened to anyone."

Catherine laughed and then wildly kicked her legs out, cutting through the air as she bellowed, "But it didn't, did it, Sue!"

Sue felt a brush of wind rush past her as Catherine's feet continued to find a target of any kind. Catherine's legs gradually stopped swinging.

Sue said again, "I'm sorry, Catherine."

They hung there, going back and forth with their words until they heard a loud sigh that made the air stand still.

Catherine took a deep swallow and closed her eyes as she listened for the sound again. Part of her wanted it to be that creepy son of a bitch from the van. She wanted to cave in that pretty face of his. Yet, all anger aside, Catherine was in no place to fight anyone, and she knew that. She didn't want to face them tied up and helpless. She had no idea what they had in store for her and Sue, but Catherine knew it wasn't good.

There were stories of people losing their minds after the outbreak and doing wicked, wicked things to other survivors. Catherine didn't believe in those stories, not because she didn't think people were capable of doing wicked things, no that wasn't the case. Catherine didn't believe anyone was going crazy; they were just showing their true colors. People are wicked deep down inside, that's what Catherine was starting to learn.

A soft mocking voice followed the sigh with, "Yap, yap, yap, yap! Don't you two ever shut up?"

Catherine's head spun to the left then to the right, causing her sack to swing wildly. "Who said that?" she asked. Sue's head popped up, and she kicked her feet in the air, as if trying to run even with the ground 3 feet below her.

"Who's there? Let us down, please!" Sue screamed out into the darkness of her sack.

The unknown voice let out a laugh, then a whole new voice joined them in the darkness. It was colder than the first.

"Faith, why did you start talking to them? Now they'll never shut up," the second voice said.

Faith groaned and pulled at her ropes. A massive creak was heard through the darkness as her ropes rubbed along the wood beam that held them. "I couldn't take it anymore!" She yelled.

Catherine fought to turn her hanging body toward the female voices that were stealing attention away from the darkness. She screamed, the burlap sack over her head causing the shouts to come off a bit muffled. "I don't know who you two bitches are but let us down now!"

Faith's mocking laughter started once again. It was like a child who was one bad word away from a timeout or an ass kicking in this case. Faith's laughter filled Catherine's head, and she didn't know who these two women were, but she already hated them. Their tones were enough to set her off.

Catherine closed her eyes and let out a scream, "Let us down now!" Just as her words hit the air, a bright light filled the room and broke through the darkness of their sacks. Catherine went still as her body slowly turned toward the light. From the left of her sack, she could hear Faith say, "Here we go with this shit again"

The other female voice shouted out, "All I wanna do is fucking sleep!"

"Ladies and gentlemen!" a familiar voice commanded the room, a soft melody playing in the background.

The song was slow at first, then it picked up. The melody became clearer and clearer as it played. Then the song hit a switch in Sue's mind and pulled her back to a dark moment in her life. A moment when she was 6 years old, lost, crying, and surrounded by clowns. It was a bad day at the circus, one that should have been forgotten long after it was done, but everyone holds onto one fear or another. Sue listened to the music and was reminded of the dirty, whiskey-smelling clown that leaned over and parted his red lips to say, "You lost, little girl?" Sue's heart pounded in her chest as the familiar voice sounded off once again.

"Boys and girls! We would like to welcome you to the grandest show on Planet Dead!"

Catherine heard a deep cackling coming from directly in front of her, and then, with a harsh yank, she was ripped from the dim light of her sack and pulled into the bright spotlight of what seemed to be a circus tent.

Catherine was eye to eye with the pretty boy from the van, but now his good looks were buried under white makeup and a dirty red wig that hung past his cartoonish red lips. The pretty boy clown was fixated on Catherine.

He leaned in close and pushed up the brim of his top hat that sat atop the dirty red mess of hair and said, "Welcome to The Rhodes Brothers Big Top Family Circus!" The clown's voice echoed throughout the night as he threw his arms back into the air to scream out over the music. "I am your ringmaster, and tonight we have for you a show sure to satisfy us all!"

The Ringmaster smiled and licked his painted lips. His hand went up to block out the bright light. "Cut the fucking light," he said.

The Ringmaster stood in a dirty, old black tuxedo, and he pulled out a red handkerchief to pat the sweat off his face, pulling a bit of white off with every dab.

"The heat's making my makeup run," he said.

The lights went out, and Catherine closed her eyes. She shook her head, then opened them to see small, orange spots take over her vision.

"Oh my God!" Sue screamed as her sack was pulled from her head, her eyes filling with images of clowns and blood.

Catherine's eyes popped open, and she finally saw what was creating the smell of shit and rotting meat in the room. Her eyes passed the large spotlight that stood in front of them and landed on the metal bleachers that normally housed an eager crowd of families who set aside an evening to see the magic of the circus.

That spot was no longer filled with smiling faces. Instead, there was blood, lots of blood and pale-skinned, gray-eyed zombies staring back at her. One zombie in the center went to leap forward with his bloodstained yellow teeth snapping, but he shot back into his seat when one of the clowns shoved a cattle prod into his chest. The spark was bright and loud, and the smell of burnt meat crawled into Catherine's nose. Catherine's eyes scanned over them; she could see they were all chained together and locked into their seats.

"What the hell is this?" Catherine's words slowly fell from her lips, and her head turned to see Sue's eyes fixed on the clown that was poking and prodding the trapped zombies.

The man was massive, the muscles that made up his shoulders bulging through his bright red and yellow clown suit. The cattle prod wasn't even necessary with the amount of force he used to push the zombies into their seats.

He had on a bright purple wig, and he held a cigar tightly between his teeth as Sue heard him growl, "Sit down, you little shits, or I'll cancel dinner time!"

The only sounds in the tent were the sparks of the prod and the ear-splitting, rapidly repetitive tone of circus music. The Ringmaster slowly walked toward the middle of the circus tent, his black boots kicking up dust as he did a little dance and twirled his cane between his fingers. The clown spun and then came to a stop before pushing up his top hat with the handle of his cane.

The large, painted smile grew on his face as his eyes came upon the female bodies hanging by their arms, hoisted in the air like some kind of backwoods deer rack. Swinging slowly, back and forth, while the Ringmaster strolled past them, pulling off the remaining two sacks.

The pale white makeup and bloodshot eyes of the Ringmaster locked onto Sue. She shook her head and closed her eyes tightly as the clown came closer to her. His hand shot out and grabbed ahold of Sue's face tightly, causing her to yelp.

The world had gone to hell. Monsters were eating people, and life as Sue knew it was over. Still, in that moment, her biggest fear was staring her in the face with a twisted, menacing smile.

"No, no, no!" Sue screamed out.

The Ringmaster let out a laugh as he looked over his

shoulder at the cattle prodding clown. "Happy!" The Ringmaster shouted, and the cattle prod slowly lowered to the clown's side.

Happy turned to face the hanging women. Catherine could see the whites of his knuckles as his fingers tightened around the handle of the prod. He pulled the cigar from his lips and tossed it back into the pack of zombies. The orange amber exploded like a firework as it smacked into a female zombie's face. The zombie's head didn't turn. It didn't even seem to blink. It just stared as Happy continued toward the women.

Happy grew larger with every step he took. Broad shoulders were connected to massive arms that seemed to be rupturing the tight, bloody clown suit. Happy stood in front of Catherine, scowling at her. He was a juggernaut of a man, and Catherine's heart raced as she saw Happy's attention leap from her to Sue.

The Ringmaster released Sue's face, placed his hand on Happy's large shoulders, and asked, "You see that, Happy? It looks like we have a little coulrophobe here!" The Ringmaster smiled at Sue before resting his head on Happy's shoulder. "It's just downright disgusting the way people treat us clowns, isn't it, Happy?"

Happy stood there and, with both hands on the cattle prod, wrung his fingers tighter and tighter around the handle. The Ringmaster turned his eyes toward the rest of the women.

"How many of you ladies are dirty little clown haters like your friend here? Huh? How many of you little whores got a problem with clowns?" The Ringmaster barked.

He gazed over the four faces that hung before him, then his red paint cracked as he smiled. "Well, no matter, we'll fish you out one by one. Happy here can smell a dirty little coulrophobe a mile away. They stink of fear, hate, and, and!" The Ringmaster snapped his finger, trying to make the word appear in his mind.

Happy's deep voice stood out over the music as he said, "Weakness. They stink of weakness."

The Ringmaster jumped up and down clapping his hands as he laughed. "Yes, yes! Weakness! Thank you, Happy." He stopped jumping and turned his head toward Sue. "You smell weak, bitch!" Bloodshot blue eyes locked on Sue. He leaned in and softly whispered into her ear, "You don't find me cute anymore, sweetie?"

Sue's eyes opened, and she shook her head quickly, trying to bat the Ringmaster away. "Catherine!" Sue screamed out.

Catherine's eyes were fixed on The Ringmaster and Happy. There was madness in the air, and as much as she wanted to blame Sue for getting them in this mess, she was more focused on getting them out of it.

Catherine's eyes made their way over to Sue. The girl had her head hung low with her eyes forced shut, trying to block out the world. Catherine could see tears dropping from Sue's cheek onto the ground below.

The Ringmaster came back into view as he walked closer to Sue once again. Sue's head shot up as she screamed , "What the hell do you want from us?!"

"Everything," the Ringmaster said as the red, cracked smile once again grew on his face. His head turned toward the two women hanging to the left of Catherine.

Catherine watched as the two women lowered their heads, as if they knew what was coming and didn't want to risk seeing even a second of it.

The Ringmaster put his hand out, standing for a moment before shouting, "Frownie!"

The Ringmaster stomped his boot into the dirt, and a skinny clown scrambled over. He bowed as he placed the handle of a long bullwhip into The Ringmaster's hand.

"Sorry, Matt." The skinny clown called Frownie said sheepishly.

Before Frownie's eyes could come up to meet The Ringmaster's, he was knocked down into the dirt by The Ringmaster's cane. Frownie rubbed the back of his head and crept away from The Ringmaster's boots.

Staring at him, The Ringmaster rolled up the whip. He spoke slowly, "What am I wearing, Frownie?"

Frownie looked at the hand that he used to rub his head. His eyes went wide as he stared at the blood on his fingertips.

"I said, what am I wearing, Frownie!" The Ringmaster shouted .

Frownie's head popped up and he crawled slowly back again, his thin knees coming up to his chest as he backed away from the madness that seemed to have taken over the night.

"The Top Hat," Frownie softly said.

The Ringmaster nodded. "That's right, and when I'm in the top hat I am no longer Matthew, but the ever-loveable Ring-master of..." The Ringmaster stopped and put his arms out wide as he yelled, "The Rhodes Brothers Big Top Family Circus!"

Catherine softly said, "You're crazy."

The Ringmaster's head turned toward Catherine, who spit out the blood that was building in her mouth onto the ground at The Ringmaster's feet. "I'm gonna be nice and I'm gonna give you the chance to let us go," Catherine said.

The Ringmaster's head turned to the side as a smile grew on his cracked face. His eyes were locked on Catherine. The moment sent a chill through Catherine. Looking into his blood-shot eyes surrounded by white makeup felt surreal. Then his eyes quickly rotated toward Sue.

The Ringmaster smiled as the whip unraveled to the ground. It was long, and it made a small thump as the leather slapped into the ground. Catherine's eyes followed the black leather as it twisted and turned until it was laying in the dirt and hay that lined the ground.

"Let you go?" The Ringmaster softly asked himself. He put his hand on his chain and slowly shook his head as his red lips parted to release another chilling laugh; it was so haunting it seemed to mix with the haunting music surrounding them. "But the fun hasn't even begun yet." He took a step back from the women. He took his top hat off and gave it a quick dusting before handing it to Frownie, who had finally got to his feet to stand next to Happy.

Happy slowly made his way over to Sue. He leaned in and took a deep sniff, running his nose along Sue's neck before grabbing her and spinning her around to look at the dark back corner of the tent.

Sue kicked her legs wildly and screeched, "Get the hell off of me! Catherine!"

Sue's screams pulled Catherine's eyes off The Ringmaster, who was rolling up his sleeves. Catherine turned her gaze toward Sue. There was no hiding it, no way of denying it; fear was written all over Sue's face as she screamed for help.

Catherine turned her head back to the Ringmaster. "Don't do this!" she pleaded.

The Ringmaster smiled as he rolled his shoulders. His dead, bloodshot eyes burned a hole into Catherine. She turned toward Sue once again. Catherine saw the tears falling down the girl's face, and she heard the deep laughter of Happy as he pulled on Sue's legs.

Catherine screamed, "Sue! Look at me!"

Sue shook her head as she tried kicking her feet to turn, but Happy held her still.

Catherine's voice came out one more time, and this time it filled the room. "Look at me!"

Sue's head turned toward Catherine, and their eyes locked on one another.

Catherine softly said, "You're gonna be okay. No matter what happens, you're gonna be okay." Catherine's head slowly turned to look over at the Ringmaster, and she screamed, "I'm gonna fucking kill you!"

. . .

*W*ith those last words, the whip thundered through the cool night air. A crack was heard, and Sue's head shot backward. Her face turned red, and she let out a chilling cry. The blood came as quickly as the whip did. Sue didn't want to look weak, so she picked her head up and slowly turned it toward Catherine.

"Look at me!" Catherine's words wrestled with Sue's screams.

Fighting through the tears, Sue wanted to say she was sorry. She was sorry for all of it, the van, the lies. That thought was dashed when another lash came clashing down onto her back. Her head snapped back and then went limp, hanging forward. A deep red covered Sue's back. There was skin and red bits of torn fabric, but most of it was blood. The blood ran down her white shirt and left dark red marks on her shorts. When the third lash came, the blood dripped into the dirt.

Catherine opened her mouth, once again screaming, "LOOK AT ME!"

Just then, the whip flew toward Catherine. It cracked in the air, barely short of her face. Catherine's eyes shot toward The Ringmaster. His smile was larger than it was before, his chest was rising and falling, and the look in his eye was some psychotic form of glee.

He roared, "No! You look at me!"

All eyes were on them now. Their heated stare-down over-took the tent. Every set of eyes waited for what would come next, every set but Sue's. She was trying her best to focus on anything but that moment. Sue pushed hard to remember a time before this, a time before the whips, before the ropes, before the zombies.

She recalled dressing up in a nice sundress and heels, twirling in front of the mirror before she was motioned to hurry along. She dug deep for that happy time, but the pain came rushing back with every breath she took. Tightening her jaw, Sue gritted her teeth as she fought to hold back tears. Through it all, she could hear The Ringmaster's words.

"This is my show. You four might be the evening's attraction, but make no mistake," He smiled as he dramatically pulled back the whip before saying, "I'm the star!"

The whip once again released and cut through the air, more forceful than the last few times he swung it. Sue's head sprung up as she let out another scream, then there were no more words; none that Sue could make out. Everything was silent. She knew Catherine was screaming something, but all she could hear was a dull buzzing in her ears.

It was the shock taking over.

Sue tried her best to stay focused on Catherine's face, but every few seconds things would blur and darken as she started fading in and out. Sue's head and body hung, motionless over the ground when the whipping finally stopped. Her back was too red to separate the skin from the fabric and blood. Blood raced down her legs and formed droplets off her white sneakers.

Catherine wanted to cry for her; she wanted to break down and hold the girl. To let her know everything would be okay, but that was a lie. Catherine knew that. She also knew that she had a new desire, a need that overshadowed everything else. It eclipsed her hunger, her fear, her will to live. This need blazed inside her like a wildfire; it was even great enough to overshadow finding her boys.

She would kill The Ringmaster.

Catherine's head turned toward The Ringmaster, who was wiping a bit of blood off his cheek. His eyes fell back onto Sue and he smiled.

"I think I got a little ahead of myself." The Ringmaster laughed and dropped the whip to the floor. "I don't want blondie too worn out." His eyes slowly made their way to Catherine. "I mean the night is still young."

Slow footsteps filled the air before Catherine heard a loud thump as Sue's body fell to the ground. The Ringmaster stood in front of Catherine, staring into her eyes through his blood-shot pools.

"Now, normally I like to share, that's just how my mother raised me, but I think I'm gonna keep you all to myself." The Ringmaster's voice washed over Catherine as his finger lightly traced down her cheek.

"When I get down from here, I'm gonna kill you," Catherine spat the words out into the night air.

The Ringmaster smiled and then broke out laughing as he looked over at Happy and Frownie, who were dragging Sue's body away. A red path of blood seemed to create a new trail of madness behind her.

"First, we're gonna have a little party up at the house with blondie, and then, when I'm done with her, I'll come back down for you."

Catherine watched as the clowns dragged Sue out of the tent. Catherine laughed.

The Ringmaster turned his head back around to look at Catherine as he asked, "What the hell is so funny?"

Catherine lowered her head and sighed. "You three." Catherine's head raised, and her eyes quickly found The Ring-master's. Her blood felt hot. She felt it rushing to her face, and she could feel the overall warmth it was giving her. It was anger. She smiled at him.

"You're all dead, and you don't even know it, just like those fucking zombies out there. It's poetic, or symbolic, or some shit like that. I just think it's funny."

. . .

*T*he Ringmaster laughed as he turned and walked out of the tent with Sue and the other two clowns. The tent flap fell back, and the women were once again alone, trapped in the madness with only each other and the moans of the zombies to pass the time.

Catherine stared at the entryway for a while. When she felt that enough time had passed, she looked up at the ropes that held her and tightened her hands around them. She felt a burning in her forearms as her body rose, but she fell back down just as quickly as she started.

The other women watched on until Faith whispered, "What are you doing, darling?"

*C*atherine didn't waste a moment to acknowledge the woman's question; there wasn't a moment worth wasting. Catherine was needed once before, looked to for answers before all this. For weeks now, she had been pushing forward based on the thought that her family needed her. Her husband, her son, they still needed her. Yet, she had no idea what was happening with them. She didn't know if they were alive or dead, but Sue was alive, and Catherine was going to make damn sure she stayed that way. In her head, she screamed, Get up! Get your ass up there!

It pulled her back to her first battle in the military: her vs. The Rope. Catherine remembered looking up at the beast, taking in how high it was, trying to push the thought of falling out of her head. The drill sergeant was screaming in the background, but the words didn't seem to push through the moment. All Catherine could remember was the sight of that rope swinging back and forth in the hot summer sun. She wrapped her hands around it and tucked her legs, and she remembered clearly, as if she had just done it yesterday, she remembered saying, <u>Get up there! Get your ass up there!</u>

*C*atherine swung her body and kicked her legs past her shoulders this time, her body turning upside down. Summer nights normally provided relief from the wicked Georgia heat, but not that night. Catherine felt as if the sun itself was resting on her shoulders, causing beads of sweat to run down her body. She didn't pay it any attention; her eyes were fixed on her boots now laced around the rope. Catherine was completely upside down now as she rolled her ankle back and forth painstakingly, hoping that would do the trick.

"Come on, motherfucker," she muttered as the two women watched her show. Nothing was happening besides the blood rushing to her head. Catherine could feel the pressure gradually building up around her eyes. Everything was upside down and splitting into two. She was just about to give up when the universe tossed her a bone in the form of a nice cool metal object falling from within her boot. She grabbed it with her hands and dropped her legs, quickly straightening her body back out. Catherine held the metal in her hands as she closed her eyes to pull herself together.

"What the fuck is that?" the other woman asked.

Catherine smirked as she slowly opened her hand, showing the little double-edge knife that she kept hidden in her boot. The women gaped at Catherine, watching her as she carefully cut through her ropes. Catherine came falling down to the ground, landing on her knees. She stayed there for a moment, letting the feeling come back to her arms and legs. The world was shit, she knew that, and it didn't take her long to learn it. In fact, she partly knew it long before the outbreak.

People didn't care about you, and the ones that did normally didn't stay around for long. They would leave or die, and you would be left in this cold state without a soul wondering how you slept at night or even caring if you woke up in the morning. The world was shit, but every so often you found people that would push through all the shit with you. Those are the people you don't let go of, those are the people you protect. Her husband, her son, they were those people, people worth dying for.

As Catherine opened her eyes and looked around the large tent, she rubbed her wrists gently one after the other as she finally got to her feet.

The two women sounded off back and forth with the same cries "Let us down!" "Get us out of here!"

Catherine put her finger to her lips and hushed the women. She walked over to Faith and swung the knife over her bright red head, cutting her down quickly. Faith landed on her ass, her dirty pink dress spreading out like a newly blooming flower among the dirt.

Catherine moved onto the next girl. The same slash above the head and the woman came falling down, except this woman landed on her feet. The woman's eyes cut over to Catherine; they were the same height and stood eye to eye. The woman had large black hair and bright hazel eyes. She wore tight blue jeans, a black jacket and a tee-shirt. Had she been a few shades darker, she could have been Catherine's stunt double. The woman turned her head from Catherine and looked toward Faith, who was slowly getting up and rubbing her ass.

"Hey, we getting out of here, or what?" Faith asked.

The dark-haired woman looked over at Faith and nodded. "Yeah," she said, then looked back over at Catherine. Her soft pink lips parted. "You coming?"

Catherine stared at her for a long moment. The woman's skin was a bit pale, more like Snow White than Count Dracula. It wasn't something to write home about, but it did seem out of place. Catherine wondered if the girl only traveled at night. That kind of movement was risky for sure, but it kept you out of the heat.

Catherine shook her head. "I got to go get Sue."

Faith raised an eyebrow and looked over at the dark-haired woman. "She's kidding, right?"

The dark-haired woman folded her arms over her chest. "I don't think she is, Faith."

The two started walking past Catherine, toward the opening of the tent. Catherine's hand shot out and grabbed ahold of the dark-haired woman's elbow. This is what the world was like now; people didn't care about your good deeds, they didn't care about how much help you need, they just cared about their needs. Catherine didn't even turn her head to look at the women.

"You're coming with me!" Catherine said as her hold on the woman's arm tightened.

Faith laughed and said, "The fuck we are."

The dark-haired woman pulled her arm free from Catherine's grasp and turned around. Catherine could see her from the corner of her eye, running her fingers through her dark black waves of hair. "I'm real grateful you saved us; we both are. I don't want you to think we're not, but your girlfriend..."

Catherine looked at the woman, who had a small shit-eating grin on her face.

"Well, she's dead. Now you can accept that and come with us, or you can end up just like her, it's up to you." The woman looked over at Faith for a moment, who was nodding, then she looked back at Catherine. "Don't play all holier than thou with us. I'm sure you've left a lot of people high and fucking dry in your life." She folded her arms over her chest. "So, what's it gonna be, Hero?"

Catherine stared at the dark-haired woman, then nodded. There wasn't anything to really think about, the world had changed around them. It got dark and allowed dark people to roam more freely than they had ever been, those kinds of people were slowly taking over this new world. They did it with force and fear. Turning a blind eye as good people, the kind of people you fought for, died off.

Catherine didn't give it a second thought either. She cocked her arm back and let her right fist fly forward, connecting with the dark-haired woman's jaw. It felt like punching through drywall, hard at first, then the jaw gave way, and the dark-haired woman tumbled to the ground.

The dark-haired woman's hands went up to her mouth, and she cried out, "What the hell!"

"What the hell is wrong with you?" Faith asked.

*C*atherine shook the tingling sensation from her knuckles. She watched Faith pull the dark-haired woman to her feet. Catherine continued to rub her knuckles. The music and moans filled the air, but the two women heard Catherine loud and clear when she finally spoke.

"I've been left behind before; it made me wonder what this world was becoming. It made me question what was wrong with me? What did they see in me that made it so easy for them to leave me to die? Those questions almost broke me, and Sue."

Catherine stopped, looking down at her knuckles. There was a pain running through her hand now, but it was nothing compared to what that dark-haired woman must have felt, or what Sue was feeling now.

Sue needed Catherine. "Sue isn't like me; those questions will kill her. So, we won't be leaving her, or anyone, behind," Catherine finished as she walked past the women toward the zombies that were moaning and pulling at their chains. "Besides, I owe that top hat wearing bitch a play date!"

Catherine wished she could mask it as payback. Part of her

wished she could have simply walked off and continued the search for her family, but Catherine knew, just like with Robert and Jordan, Sue was one of those people you didn't let go of. She was one of the people you protected.

A zombie leaped toward Catherine, snapping its jaws and pulling her out of her thoughts. She walked slowly forward until they were face to bloody face. She could see the zombie was missing one of its eyes, and a large hole in its neck pushed out dark red blood and rancid meat as it kept pushing forward.

Catherine stared at the zombie until the blood from his head splashed across her chest as the dark-haired woman slammed a hammer into the man's skull. Catherine turned to look at her.

"I fucking hate the circus," the dark-haired woman said as she leaned down to pull the hammer out of the man's head. "So, what's the plan?"

Catherine glanced at Faith, who was sitting on the floor with her knees to her chest, slowly rocking.

"Is she gonna be okay?" Catherine asked.

The dark-haired woman looked over at Faith, and she waved her hand while rolling her eyes. "Yeah, she's just easily spooked, that's all."

Catherine looked at Faith, then at the chained-up zombies who were fighting to be free. "And this doesn't spook you?" Catherine asked.

The dark-haired woman smiled and shook her head. "This?" She looked back at the monsters and said, "There's far worse out there than this." The woman's hand came out with a smile. "Tennessee."

Catherine stared at Tennessee with a blank look on her face. "That's your name?"

Tennessee nodded, walking past Catherine. "It is now." Tennessee walked over to Faith, and got down on one knee. "Come on Faith, time to put our big girl panties on."

Catherine didn't know what to make of the two. She wasn't sure if she could trust them, but if she was going to get this done and make it out alive, she needed them. "My name's Catherine, Catherine Briggs," she said

"Okay, Mrs. Briggs. What's the plan?" Tennessee asked as she walked back over with Faith in tow.

Catherine smiled; she hadn't been called Mrs. Briggs in forever. She never knew how much she missed hearing it until that moment. It made her feel connected with her husband once again. She looked over at Faith and Tennessee.

"First things first, we need weapons!" Catherine turned around, and her eyes came back onto the zombies who were fighting to be free, fighting to taste a little blood. "And we need them!" Her caramel finger pointed at their audience of the dead.

Tennessee smiled and bumped Faith with her hip, laughing. "I think I like her," she said.

Faith covered her mouth with her hand and mumbled, "I think I'm gonna be sick."

5

IF I WERE SURROUNDED ...WOULD I STAND A CHANCE

PLANET DEAD

"Get her up!" The Ringmaster's commands echoed throughout the summer night.

Sue used to look forward to nights like those. The kind of nights when a cool breeze gave you a break from the burning heat that most Georgia summers provided, carrying that sweet hidden scent of the countryside. Yes, it was nights like those that Sue's heart longed for, but, as she felt the cold touch of dirty hands grabbing at her and dragging her body through the summer night, all Sue longed for now was this night to end.

Blood ran from open wounds with every small movement, but she couldn't feel it, not in the way she thought she should. No, all she felt was cold, wet, and numb. A dull tingle ran up and down her back which caused Sue to hold her eyes tightly shut. Sue was fading in and out; one moment she saw the ropes of the tent, then darkness. The next moment she saw the night sky in all its bright, beautiful glory, and then darkness again. Sue felt like she was lost in a dream, but as her eyes flickered back open, she awoke to a nightmare. A quick river of red made its way along the old wooden floor where Sue's head lay.

Sue pushed up slightly, then dropped down. She could feel the pain now; it was like razors continually dragging down her back. Sue bit down on her lower lip and prayed the shock would come back, that her body would go numb once again. Sue heard laughter around her as she pushed again, but her head raised for only a short moment before it came flying back down into the blood.

The sound of her head slamming into the floor caused the three clowns to turn their attention toward Sue. A red smile grew on The Ringmaster's face as he slowly made his way over to her.

"Well, well, well! Look who finally decided to join the party!" His shouts rang throughout Sue's head.

She closed her eyes as she forced her body to roll over to her side. Her blonde hair mopped up the blood covering the ground around her. Sue finally got to her knees, only to feel a hard blow to her back, sending her crashing back down into the blood.

Blood covered the side of her face and mixed in with tears as she tried to push herself up once again, but there was no escaping The Ringmaster's black boot that pinned her to the floor.

The Ringmaster leaned down, resting his arms on his knee. He whispered to Sue, "Where you off to, honey?"

Sue slowly moved her hands toward her back, but they were quickly slapped away by The Ringmaster. The large black boot came up, and she felt the weight lift off her lower back. Sue took that opportunity to muster every bit of strength in her. She shot up and raced to a nearby open window. The blood and tears blurred her vision, but she could feel the cool breeze blowing past the curtains in the room.

Sue threw her hands out, grabbing hold of the white silk curtains. She didn't fool herself into believing she was safe, she didn't lie to herself thinking she could leap from another window and make it out okay. Sue didn't have hope, all she had was the need to be free. Dirty hands wrapped around Sue's hair and dragged her down to the blood-soaked floor once again. Sue realized freedom wasn't a possibility, and her life as she knew it was over.

There was no escaping this…

"Pick her the fuck up!" The Ringmaster shouted.

There was no overcoming this…

"Put her in the trunk," The Ringmaster continued.

This was evil…

You don't escape evil! You don't overcome evil!

You just lay there, broken and scared, and you pray it gets tired of your tears.

Happy and Frowny wrapped their hands tightly around any body part of Sue's they could grab. She felt the pain in her arm, her ankle, and then all at once in her back as they dropped her into a small wooden trunk. Sue's hands went over her face as she tried to clear away the blood from her eyes. When her vision cleared, she saw The Ringmaster standing over her once again. His face was covered with dirty pale white paint, there were black rings around his eyes and bright red lipstick that was madly drawn over his lips. The lipstick made his teeth pop as he smiled at her; they were pure white and straight. Something Sue found odd in the back of her mind, but it was a thought that couldn't make it past the fear that took over the forefront of her mind.

"You're cute. Sweet even," The Ringmaster said.

The Ringmaster placed his hands on the large lid, and let out a laugh. "You got that girl next door look, you know that? The one you fall in love with but forget about once you go to college and discover drugs and blow jobs."

The Ringmaster looked over at his brothers, who had pulled up seats by the doorway, then his eyes made their way back to Sue. "It's nice to know that some things haven't fully changed," he said as his hand went toward Sue's face. Sue spun her head back and forth, but his fingers locked onto her cheeks, forcing her lips to pucker.

The Ringmaster smiled and said, "Something happened to the world. People lost their minds! And to be honest with you, I think it's glorious." That bright red smile got wider as The Ringmaster leaned into the trunk until he was face-to-face with Sue. "You can see it, can't you, blondie? People call it insanity, but it's really just human nature. We can only evolve so much, 'til we come crashing back down into the pit."

The Ringmaster broke out laughing as he squeezed Sue's cheeks harder, leaving deep red marks where his fingers were. He kept his hand on the lid of the trunk as his laughing died and his bloodshot eyes fixed upon Sue once again.

"So, tell me! How deep in the pit are you?" He smiled as he softly whispered into Sue's face, brushing his lip against hers, "How deep?" The Ringmaster let the words hang in the air for a moment, then leaned closer and kissed Sue, forcing his lips onto hers.

When his head came back, Sue locked her eyes with his. He smiled and slowly released her. "Speechless?" The Ringmaster asked. Laughing, he looked at his brothers and said, "I have that effect on women, don't I, boys?"

The words sent a rush of emotions through Sue's body. She thought it would be a chill, that funny little rush of fear that fills up your body, but it wasn't. What went through Sue was a blazing heat. Her skin was hot, and the vein on the side of her head pulsated. What went through Sue was rage.

Sue shot up and let out a scream that came from deep in her stomach, "I'm gonna fucking kill you!"

Her words were met with a laugh and the slamming of the large wooden lid onto her head. Sue's body dropped back into the trunk, and she held her forehead, trying her best to hold back the blood that spilled out.

Sue heard metal knocking against the wood of the trunk, and then a loud click. She listened as footsteps walked away from her. She sat up and pushed the lid up as much as she could. It was locked, but she could partly see through the crack.

Sue's eyes focused past the darkness of the truck to the three clowns in the room. "What you gonna do with her?" Sue heard the soft question come from the lips of the smallest clown, who was in the process of cleaning off his makeup with a dirty rag.

Frownie almost fell off his chair when he was slapped on the back, the echoing sound followed by a loud laugh.

"What the hell do you think we're gonna do with her, huh Frownie?" Happy asked with a smile. He walked out of Sue's view, but she could still hear his deep voice as he said, "The freaks have to eat! We got to eat!"

Happy's matter-of-fact tone gave Sue a chill. He spoke like kidnapping and murdering were merely a part of their lives now. Sue's eyes rested on Frownie as he stared down at the floor. He bit his lip and shook his head slowly as his hand formed into a fist. There was a long moment of silence that allowed Happy's words to take over the room. Sue was about to drop back down to the base of the trunk when she heard that soft voice once again. "That's not my name."

Frownie kept his head hung low, looking at the dirt that covered his white sneakers. He rubbed one foot over the other, trying to push some of the dirt away, yet it wasn't going anywhere. It was a dark brown powder that was all over the floor of the tent, and with all their late night *"shows,"* it covered everything else. There wasn't anything he could remember seeing that didn't have that brown tint. No matter how hard he rubbed, he just couldn't get it off. Frownie went to clean it off with his finger when he felt his face being lifted by Happy's large hands.

Happy was fast, faster than a man his size should have been.

He rushed from one side of the room to the other before Sue could blink. Frownie's feet kicked as Happy picked him up slightly off the ground by his cheeks.

"That's your name now, you little shit!" Happy's fingers dug into Frownie's cheeks, then he tossed Frownie into the wall and pointed a finger at him. "We should have left your ungrateful ass behind!"

"Now, now, boys. There's no need for us to act like animals, now is there?" The calm voice came from around the corner of the trunk.

Sue's eyes scanned the room, but when she came to the corner, she was eye to eye with the monster who was running this wicked show. Smiling wide, Sue saw the cracks growing along the red lipstick as his white teeth got longer and longer.

"You enjoying the show?" The Ringmaster hissed.

Sue couldn't pull her eyes away from him. The sight of him kept her still; it sent a wave of fear through her body. Her heart raced, and she could feel the tears building back up behind her eyes. The Ringmaster moved his hand to the lid of the trunk, and Sue felt it pushing down against her head once again. She put her hands up to fight back against the force.

It was a small show of force The Ringmaster was using, but Sue used everything she had, and it wasn't worth a damn. Sue watched as the crack became smaller and smaller. She almost gave up all hope until she heard a voice from the other side of the room.

"That's enough, Matthew!" Frownie's voice echoed. It wasn't soft and questionable like before. No, this time it was strong and commanding.

Everyone's eyes turned toward Frownie. Happy leaped forward until he was standing right in front of Frownie, who was sitting with his head down, staring at his dirty shoes.

The Ringmaster slowly stood to his feet and put his hand up. "It's okay, Daniel." he said, causing Happy to take a step back. "Clearly, Adam has something he would like to get off his chest." The Ringmaster pulled up a chair and swung his leg over it. Sitting backwards, he leaned forward and smiled. "So, tell us Adam. What's on your mind?"

Sue's eyes went to Adam, who looked more like a normal young man than a crazed clown now that he cleaned off most of the makeup. As her eyes rested on him, she took him in. He wasn't scary or evil; in fact, he looked like any other guy she would have seen in class or at a party. The dirty rag came down from his face, and Sue could see the soft glow of his light green eyes. Adam tossed the rag to the floor and cleared his tousled blonde locks from his face. Sue kept her hands up, holding up the lid as Adam's head slowly turned. Their eyes met, and then his gaze went toward his brother Matthew, the monster Sue will forever know as The Ringmaster.

"I don't understand why we keep doing this. It was one thing when we were hurting for food, but now! We don't need to do this," Adam finally said.

The Ringmaster smiled and nodded before turning his head toward Daniel. "You hear that, big brother? Little brother doesn't understand." The Ringmaster said it softly and let out a light laugh, but Daniel wasn't laughing.

He stood staring down his brother with chalky white makeup mixed in with his black beard. Sue watched the mountain of a man as his fingers slowly cracked, forming his hands into two large fists.

Adam could feel his older brother's eyes on him and did his best not to turn his head toward Daniel's direction.

"I just mean we aren't trapped anymore; we can travel. We can find food, we can survive without, without—" Adam's hands went over his face, and he sighed.

Whatever the matter was, it seemed as if Adam battled with it for some time now. He was sweating, and while his words were clear and defiant, there was a bit of fear hidden away in his tone.

The Ringmaster nodded and looked back at the trunk, and Sue quickly dropped the lid. Balling up inside the trunk, Sue heard footsteps once again, and then the voice of The Ringmaster echoed throughout the little trunk.

"Well, sweetheart, looks like you got my brother all flustered," The Ringmaster's glare turned back toward Adam as he continued, "I mean, that must be it, right? Blondie giving you the butterflies?"

Sue heard metal knocking against the trunk once again as The Ringmaster softly said, "You want a little taste?"

Adam shook his head and shot up out of his seat toward his brother but was pushed into the wall by Daniel.

"Fuck you, Matthew!" Adam shouted.

The Ringmaster laughed, and Sue started to sweat as she braced her feet against the lid of the trunk. She bit down on her lip as the slashes on her back pressed against the wood. The Ringmaster rushed toward his brother, swinging the chair across the room. "Fuck me?" The Ringmaster shouted, scowling at Adam.

The Ringmaster's chest rose and fell as the white makeup on his face cracked to reveal a twisted smile. His white face turned up toward the dim light in the room. It was a silent moment, the kind where all you can hear is your heart beating.

Sue's heart wasn't just beating, it was pounding out of her chest. She didn't know what was going on. All she knew was she was bleeding and locked in a trunk. So, no matter who opened that lid, she planned on giving them hell.

The Ringmaster's face came down with a large smile, which was enhanced and even more terrifying due to the red lipstick covering his face. The Ringmaster winked at Daniel and the large man quickly grabbed a hold of Adam, slamming him into the old wooden door.

Adam kicked his legs, trying his hardest to get a foot back on the ground, but it was useless. Daniel had him up in the air once again. This time, Adam could feel his lungs fighting for air as Daniel held his throat tightly. The Ringmaster slowly walked over to Adam. He leaned down and picked up his cane from the floor.

"No, no, little brother. You won't be fucking anything tonight, but we will be," The Ringmaster said with a laugh.

The cane came out over Daniel's shoulder and slowly pushed into Adam's face. The cold gold metal pressed against Adam's cheek, helping his face turn a darker red than it already was. Adam fought, and he would have slapped the cane away, but he was too busy using his hands to keep Daniel from strangling him.

"You wanna know what we're gonna do with her? Huh? I'll tell you! We're gonna do whatever the fuck we want with her," The Ringmaster said and then smiled before he continued. "We'll do whatever the fuck we want all night, and then I'll kill her." The Ringmaster's head turned to the side as he stared at his little brother. He made a sad face and said, "Not because we're hungry, not because she's a threat. No, no, no! I'll kill her because I can!" The Ringmaster leaned into the cane with great force, then pulled it back, leaving a large red mark on Adam's face.

"That's just how it is, little brother, and that's just how it will always be." The Ringmaster looked over his shoulder at the trunk once again.

Footsteps echoed through the wood as Sue's feet pressed along the lid.

"Don't act like we haven't done this before," The Ringmaster said as he pulled the key out of his pocket.

Sue felt her heart pounding against her rib cage. Her eyes widened as the lid lifted. Sue kicked her feet with all her force, slamming the lid into The Ringmaster's face.

Sue sprung up and balled her fist. Her heart was still pounding, and her back still burned from her last beating, but she wasn't going to just sit and wait to die, not like this. Sue's right fist flew toward The Ringmaster, but it was all for nothing as the monster took hold of her small balled up hand and pulled Sue close to him.

"Aw, somebody wants to play rough?" The Ringmaster asked with a smile as he turned his head to spit out a bit of blood. He turned to his brothers as he said, "Daniel, give Adam a nice seat for the show." The Ringmaster licked his bloody lips as he turned back to face Sue. "He's not gonna want to miss this."

Sue's eyes were filled with tears now. She was pushing and pulling, but she was too weak. The Ringmaster leaned in closer to Sue until she could feel the heat coming from his lips. His hand went onto his belt buckle, and Sue closed her eyes.

"What the fuck's going on?"

The Ringmaster's shouting caused Sue's eyes to pop open, but when they did, it was to total darkness. The lights in the room had gone out and there were loud bangs coming from downstairs. The Ringmaster swung his head toward Daniel.

"Go see what that is!" he hissed through the darkness.

Sue could hear the big man stumbling around, trying to find his way through the blackness of the room. Sue laughed; it started out quietly, then it grew. It was a broken set of cackles that was somewhat haunting to hear in the darkness.

The Ringmaster grabbed her hair and bent her head backward. "What the fuck is so funny?"

Sue smiled in the darkness as she whispered, "You're dead and you don't even know it."

6

STILL AFRAID

PLANET DEAD

"*This* was a dumb plan!" Tennessee screamed from behind Catherine.

Catherine turned her head to see the two women hauling ass behind her. She wanted to scream "shut the hell up" or "this is gonna work," but as her eyes moved past Tennessee and Faith, they found the fast-moving pack of zombies approaching them. Catherine thought it best to keep her head forward, her legs moving, and her thoughts on happier times. Any time other than this moment would have worked.

"Just keep moving!" Catherine finally shouted as they sprinted toward the old farmhouse that stood at the top of the hill. As they rushed through the tall grass of the hillside, that house seemed like their safe haven, the only thing to save them from their misguided attempt at an ambush. Yet, even with this pretty picture of their newly found safe zone, Catherine knew once they got through those doors, there was gonna be a whole other world of problems.

The burning started off small, a slight annoying itch on her foot. Then it grew beyond her toes, to her calf, then her thighs.

As she felt the burning take over both her legs and lungs, Catherine immediately wished she hadn't canceled that gym membership last year. She wished she had stayed in fighting shape like when she was in the Army, but sadly late-night pizza and movie nights with the family sounded better than laps in the pool.

As her mind came across that long-forgotten memory of watching random comedies with her boys, she found herself pushing past the burning. Catherine kept her eyes forward, focused on the door of the farmhouse. She told herself she was racing toward her family. She told herself if she didn't make it to that door, she would never see them again. A fire started up in Catherine, and she sped up the hill faster.

"Keep fucking moving!" Catherine shouted.

The three women fought their way up with Catherine leading the charge and poor Faith falling behind. With every step she took, she could see Tennessee and Catherine taking two or even three steps more. They seemed to be built for this, built to survive, built to fight, but not Faith.

Long before the dead started roaming the earth, Faith knew she wasn't meant for a long life. She came from a broken home; her mother had walked out on them when she was five. The woman packed one bag and kissed her daughter on the cheek saying, "Be good, Faith," and that was it. She ran, leaving Faith alone with a monster for a father. Faith's life was just one hellish beating for thirteen years until Faith found a way out.

It was an escape that came in the form of a young soldier named Mark. Faith had gone to school with Mark and never really thought much about him until he showed up in his Army workout uniform. It wasn't the uniform that got her heart racing; it was everything that came with it. Mark was going places, far off places away from the monster that lived in her house. Faith thought Mark could keep her safe, so they got married. She was full of hope as she unpacked her life to start a new one in Georgia, far from the monster in Texas. Over time, Faith realized she had just traded one monster for another.

With every hit Mark delivered, Faith knew she wasn't built for a long life, and as she watched the farm house moving out of her sight and the ground coming closer to her face, she knew for a fact she wasn't built to survive, wasn't built to fight. She just wasn't built for any of this. Faith rolled over onto her back and watched as the zombies raced toward her.

"Oh my God!" Faith screamed. Her voice was high and cracking, a sound that cut through the night, causing both Catherine and Tennessee to turn around quickly.

Faith closed her eyes in hopes that if she didn't see her fate coming, it wouldn't hurt as bad. It was an old trick she developed with her father and perfected with her husband. Faith would close her eyes tightly, waiting for that chilling sound of a fist or an open hand hitting a body part, and then pain would follow. This time, she was listening for ripping or teeth tearing into skin. Yet, all she heard were feet slamming into the ground, and all she felt was her legs burning and her wrist cramping. When she opened her eyes, she saw the zombies falling farther and farther away as the grass around her zipped past her dress. Faith leaned her head back to see Catherine holding onto her left hand and Tennessee holding onto her right. The two women dragged Faith with everything they had.

"We're almost there," Catherine pushed the words out of her mouth, and Faith closed her eyes once again. They were risking their lives for her.

They could have left her, turned away and acted as if they didn't see anything, like so many had done before. Yet, they saw her at her weakest and picked her up or dragged her in this case. She didn't know how it made her feel to know everyone she trusted or loved worked their hardest to break her, and here were these women she hardly knew working their hardest to keep her alive. When this was all done, Faith was going to have to rethink the meaning of love, that was for sure.

They were racing toward hope, and with the sound of the wooden steps creaking from the weight of Catherine's boot, they realized they had finally made it. Both Catherine and Tennessee dropped Faith's arms at the same time.

"Get the fuck up, Faith!" Tennessee shouted without even looking down at the woman or offering a helping hand.

Tennessee darted toward the front door only to have a hand slap into her chest.

"Hold on," Catherine whispered.

Tennessee slapped Catherine's hand away. "We don't have time to hold on," Tennessee hissed back, causing Catherine to turn to look at the zombies that were just feet away from the front steps.

"We can't just go in through the front. We don't know what the hell is waiting for us," Catherine whispered as she walked around the wraparound porch.

Faith stood up to watch Tennessee roll her eyes and quickly rush behind Catherine. Both women moved swiftly, hugging the walls and trying to stay below the windows. Faith hesitated , turning her head to the side, and then she took off running along the house.

Catherine's head shot forward. "What the fuck are you doing?" she shouted as softly as she could.

They watched Faith run through the grass. She moved quickly, darting past a wooden shed, then past one of the pillars of the house, and then she was gone. Catherine and Tennessee looked at each other, puzzled.

Tennessee murmured, "Where'd she go?"

Catherine shrugged her shoulders. They cautiously moved toward the porch railing. Catherine's hand went to touch the wood but stopped when Faith's head popped up.

"You two coming?" Faith whispered.

Catherine looked over the railing to see two large doors and steps leading down into the house's cellar.

Tennessee smiled and stood up. "And here I was thinking you were useless," she said as she tossed her legs over the railing, one after the other.

Catherine stood up and saw the zombies making their way up the steps. She put one hand on the railing to steady her body as she leaped over, landing on the grass below. The three women raced down the steps. Catherine was behind them as she pulled the two doors shut. She held them together in her hands and looked back at Faith.

"Good job. Now find me something to keep these doors shut," Catherine said.

Faith smiled for a moment before turning and searching through the dark cellar, moving slowly to avoid tripping over anything.

Tennessee put her hand in her pocket and then pulled out a lighter. Her thumb rolled down along the metal, creating a flame to brighten up a small area in front of her face. "Where is it?" she said softly.

Faith's head turned toward Tennessee's voice. "Where's what?" she asked.

Tennessee ignored Faith as she continued to search carefully throughout the cellar. Her eyes moved from the walls to the ceiling, routing back and forth before she said, "Got it!"

The lights of the cellar went on, and Faith jumped back. She was going to scream, but Tennessee shot toward her, slapping her hand over Faith's mouth. Both women's eyes widened as they walked backwards toward the steps they had run down moments ago.

Looking over her shoulder as she held the doors for dear life, Catherine shouted, "Hello! What the hell are you two doing?"

Tennessee pointed. Catherine's eyebrow went up, and her fingers fell from the door handles as her eyes followed Tennessee's finger to four bodies hanging in the middle of the room, much like they once were, but these four women were upside down. Their throats were cut, and blood overflowed the buckets that laid under each of their heads. Once their eyes took in the sight, their noses took in the smell. It ran up Catherine's nose, burning every inch of it, then raced down to her stomach and tried to force all of its contents out; with each bit of air that went into her lungs came that scent that screamed at her body to purge itself.

While Catherine fought to hold it together, Faith let it all fall apart as she threw up in Tennessee's hand.

"Oh, fuck nah!" Tennessee exclaimed, pulling her hand back.

"I'm so sorry," Faith said as she dropped to her knees.

Catherine's eyes were just as wide as the others, but from the corner of her eye, she could see the cellar door slowly opening. "Get me something!" she shouted as she spun around to hold the door shut once again, this time feeling the force behind it fighting to get it open.

Tennessee shook the vomit from her fingertips as she looked around the room. Her light brown eyes came upon a large crowbar sitting in the corner of the room. She ran toward it and quickly scooped it up. It wasn't until she passed it to Catherine that Tennessee realized it was covered in blood. Catherine pushed it between the handles and took a step back from the doors that were now being frantically pulled at. Catherine looked down at her blood-covered hands, then back at the bodies hanging in the room.

"This isn't gonna hold. We need to move fast," Catherine pushed the words out, trying her best to pull her thoughts away from the evil that had occurred in that room.

Faith stared at the pool of vomit on the floor, refusing to look up. "That's what they did with them. That's why they never came back," she said softly.

Tennessee nodded, looking over at Faith as she said, "Come on, let's go."

Catherine cleaned the blood off her hands by rubbing it into her blue jeans. She shook her hands and then rolled her shoulders before walking toward the steps that lead to the upper level of the house. Her foot went on the first step, and then she felt a hand on her shoulder pull her back.

"What the hell do you think you're doing?" Tennessee asked, crossing her arms over her chest.

Catherine rolled her eyes. "I'm gonna go get Sue, or did you forget why we're here?"

Tennessee looked up at the top of the steps for a moment and then looked back at Catherine. "I came here to kill some clowns, and since your last plan almost got us killed..." Tennessee stopped and looked over at the bodies, "I don't want to end up looking like these bitches!"

Faith shook her head. "Don't call them that!" she cried out, and Tennessee sighed, closing her eyes for a moment before opening them and looking back at Catherine.

"All I'm saying is, we need another plan," Tennessee said.

Catherine looked at the top of the steps. She didn't have a plan. She knew letting the zombies go would make for an easier escape; she knew that she needed to get into the house; she knew she had to save Sue; but, aside from kicking down some doors, she didn't really have a plan.

Catherine turned back to the dead bodies hanging in the room and nodded. "You're right!" she said.

"Thank you, so let's come up with something—" Tennessee was cut off as Catherine ran to the bodies.

Catherine's arm went under the head of one of the dead

girls. She tried not to look the girl in the eyes, but she couldn't really avoid it. The bright blue just seemed to stare right into Catherine's soul. Before she knew it, she was looking over the whole body. She noticed bits of it missing, like large chunks had been torn away, no cutaway. They weren't tears, like you would see with an animal or zombie attack, they were clean cuts into the girl's body.

The smell, the cuts, the blood, it was all spinning around in Catherine's head now, and she came to two conclusions: one, she needed to get Sue out of here, and two, those clowns needed to die. Catherine leaned into the body, causing blood to rub up along her cheek. She pulled her hand back; it came back covered in blood and with a bloodstained wooden bat wrapped in her fingers.

"There isn't time for a great plan," Catherine said, getting to her feet. Her eyes were locked on the baseball bat in her hand. She focused on the blood stains for a moment, then she looked back at the bodies as she continued, "Even if there were time, I don't think there is a good plan for something like this. There are no cops to call, no prisons to hold them in." Catherine sighed. "No judge and no jury. There's just us." Catherine turned around slowly to look at Faith and Tennessee, who were now standing at the bottom of the steps staring at her.

Catherine slammed the baseball bat into her open hand and smiled as she said, "It's just us and them, so the plan is simple. Grab something, head the fuck up the stairs, and make sure we're the only ones walking out when it's all said and done."

Tennessee nodded and walked over to a table to the left of the stairs. "All you had to say was you didn't have a plan," Tennessee said while searching through some boxes on the table.

Faith smirked as she walked past Catherine, who was

shaking her head. "They have throwing knives?" Faith asked, and before she knew it, Tennessee appeared by her side.

"I'll take those," Tennessee said.

Faith shook her head and said, "No, I found them!"

The two women went back and forth, but before Catherine could tell them to shut the hell up, a loud bang sounded, followed by screaming.

Tennessee grabbed one of the knives. "We'll both take one, but when this is over, the set is mine."

Faith nodded and grabbed one of the knives. Slowly, they made their way up the steps, one behind the other with Catherine leading the way. Catherine held her bat tightly, the blood on her hands mixing with the blood on the tape of the wooden handle. The zombies were getting louder outside.

Catherine wanted to believe they wouldn't notice, that they would just think it was from the tent or some random zombies that came along, but all that was just wishful thinking. Catherine wanted to believe she still had the element of surprise, but as she pushed open the door at the top of the steps, she knew the element of surprise was long gone. She had to go into this believing they knew she was coming.

Catherine turned her head to the left, then to the right as she stepped through the doorway. She peered around the corner into the kitchen, then looked back at Tennessee and Faith. "All clear," Catherine said softly.

Tennessee and Faith came onto the main floor, each gripping a knife. Tennessee's knife was held out horizontally in front of her face, so that the blade acted as a barrier to whatever were to come out from the corners of the house. This also allowed her to have one hand free should she need to open a door, throw a punch, or do any other number of things. Faith was a whole other story; she had both her hands wrapped tightly on the knife, her knuckles turning a shade whiter than the rest of her body. Faith held it out pointy end first as she came around the corner. This would allow her to stab anything that was in front of her, which wasn't a bad tactic when you knew what was in front of you.

A large staircase came into view as they turned the corner with their shoulders pressed against the wall. Catherine heard yelling coming from the top of the steps. She held her bat at the ready as she moved toward the sounds. Her foot hit the bottom step, and she looked down at it. She saw smears of blood running up the staircase.

She looked back at Tennessee and Faith, giving them a nod as she said, "Let's go."

When she turned back to take another step, the room went pitch black. Catherine heard a faint moan in the background. She turned to see where it was coming from when Tennessee came crashing into her.

"You fucking bitch!" Tennessee shouted as she landed on Catherine.

Laying on the bottom step, Catherine quickly pushed Tennessee off of her. "What the hell is your problem?" she whispered.

Tennessee's hand went to her lower back, her fingers running over the wet and warm burning sensation that was the source of her reaction. "She fucking stabbed me!" Tennessee whispered back.

Faith stood shaking with the knife in her hand. "I'm so sorry, I'm so sorry, Tiff—" Before Faith could finish her words, Tennessee placed the cool metal of her knife against Faith's cheek.

"You're not, but if you keep it up, you'll be real sorry," Tennessee said.

Catherine slowly stood to her feet and looked at Faith with her red cheeks and tears building up in her eyes. Faith was shaking, and Catherine watched her knees move back and forth for a moment before pulling Tennessee back and putting her hand on Faith's shoulder.

"You stay down here and make sure those things don't get in the house."

Faith's eyes were still fixed on Tennessee, who had lowered the knife when Catherine got to her feet.

"Okay, Faith? Just stay down here," Catherine softly reinforced one last time before looking at Tennessee, whose eyes were fixed on Faith.

Tennessee looked over at Catherine and coldly said, "What?"

Catherine stood with her bat at the ready, eyeing Tennessee. Catherine didn't trust her, which wasn't odd because she didn't really trust anyone these days, but she knew for a fact that there was just something off about Tennessee. Her overreactions were warning signs during more normal times. Yet, during a period like this, people with warning signs were kings and queens. Able to do and act while others questioned and related. Tennessee rolled her eyes, which was beginning to seem like her trademark move as she started for the steps.

"Come on, let's go get your girlfriend," Tennessee said into the darkness.

Catherine watched her only for a short moment before she started up the stairs behind her. The duo were only halfway up the staircase when Catherine turned to look back at Faith. She felt for the woman, much like she felt for Sue. There were just two kinds of people left in the world: the survivors and the dead. Catherine knew which one she wanted to be; she just didn't know which one the world saw. Her eyes focused on Faith through the darkness.

She was standing there with the knife resting in her hand by her side. Catherine wanted to put on a smile to let her know it was going to be okay; she wanted to hug her and let her know it was alright. Catherine wanted to do a lot of things, but like Tennessee said before, there wasn't much time for anything. She needed to get herself ready for what was coming. Her head turned back toward the steps, and Catherine could hear loud laughing coming from the room to the right of the staircase. It sounded like a woman's voice, and as Catherine stepped closer, the voice became more and more clear.

"Sue?" she questioned softly.

Tennessee held her knife up and slowly made her way toward the door. She looked over at Catherine, who was standing tall with the bat ready for a massive swing, while Tennessee remained hunched over. One hand holding the knife, the other making its way for the cool metal of the doorknob.

"One," Tennessee let the words out softly. She was risking her life for a person she had only known for an hour, diving into the fires of this madness to ensure Sue made it out. "Two." All because Catherine wanted to finally play hero. The thought angered Tennessee, and she bottled up that anger for what was to come.

Catherine held the bat firmly in her hands as she thought there must be more to Tennessee. Catherine was sure anyone who was willing to fight alongside you had to have some bit of good in their heart. Tennessee could have left, escaped when she had the chance, but she didn't. Tennessee wasn't anywhere near the level of being trusted or being a friend, but as Catherine stood behind her waiting for that final word before they blasted into whatever Hell awaited them, she knew Tennessee was no threat to her.

"Three." The words came out soft and slowly, and the whole event seemed to move in slow motion.

That was until the door flew open, pulling Tennessee along with it. Tennessee slammed into the floor, right in the middle of the doorway. The knife quickly skated across the wooden floor.

As Tennessee started to get her legs back under her, she could see Daniel's dirty black boots come into view. Her eyes slowly made the long journey up to Daniel's face.

"What the hell!" Daniel let the words rush from his lips like a roar, the statement was so powerful it caused everyone's eyes to focus on the doorway.

The large clown wasted no time reacting to their unwanted party guest. His boot came flying into Tennessee's chest, sending the woman into the banister of the staircase. Tennessee's body crashed into the wood, sending some of the rods falling down the steps. Catherine's head spun right to Daniel, the large clown ripped his purple wig off his head. Catherine's fingers tightened around the handle of the wooden bat; she could feel the cold bloodstained tape rub along her fingers as she stood with her legs slightly apart. She was getting ready for whatever attack the large man had in store for her.

As Daniel's head turned toward her a voice shouted, "Stop fucking around and kill those bitches!"

Catherine didn't have to see the bastard to know the voice belonged to The Ringmaster. She took a step back slowly as Daniel started taking steps toward her, rubbing his knuckles one hand at a time as he glared at Catherine through the black rings of makeup that surrounded his eyes.

"You heard the man. Now how about we just put down the bat like a nice little girl?" Daniel said with a smile as he took another step closer to Catherine. Her slow backward footsteps came upon the edge of the staircase. "Come on, little girl, just..."

Catherine hung her head as she said softly, "I'm not a little girl."

Daniel stopped moving, and a smile grew on his face. "Oh no?" he asked.

Catherine's head shot up. "No!"

With that word, the bat came swinging down low toward Daniel's knees, but before it could connect with any bones or cause any damage, it slammed into Daniel's open hand. The giant's smile grew larger as he slowly pulled on the bat, holding a tight grip on the wood. No matter how hard Catherine shook it, she couldn't break it free. Her feet pulled along the dirty bloodstained floor.

Catherine's forearms burned, her legs tightened, and she pulled. She did her best not to look up at him, to avoid the large paint-covered smile as much as she could. But as the toes of her boots connected with his, signaling the end of their tug-of-war, Catherine could do nothing else but look up at him.

"I'm not gonna ask again. Give it to me, bitch," Daniel growled into Catherine's face.

She could taste the man's breath in her mouth. It was a mix of vodka and meat; what kind of meat, Catherine didn't want to know.

Catherine's grip on the bat began to weaken. From some-where below her, she heard a weak laugh. "You want it? Here!" Before she could process the voice, Catherine felt the bat release, causing her to stumble back a few steps.

Daniel's eyes widened. Catherine could see every bit of white, every small red vein that made up the road map to his black soul. Their eyes locked on one another, trapped in that moment of shock, but Daniel's eyes broke first. He moved them slowly toward his bloody boot. Catherine's eyes quickly followed, and what she saw was a gleeful Tennessee smiling with a bit of blood at the corner of her mouth.

Tennessee's hands were wrapped tightly around the handle of her throwing knife, the knife buried deeply into the middle of Daniel's boot. She looked up at the mountain of a man and laughed, letting go of the knife. "Bitch!"

Daniel let out a scream of his own, but it was short-lived as Catherine swung the bat to the back of the large man's head, knocking him to the floor next to Tennessee. Tennessee shot up to her feet and leaned over to pull the knife out. She twisted and turned it, causing Daniel to shake with every move.

"Come on, come home to mama!" Tennessee said.

"You two whores don't seem to know your place, do you?"

That voice grabbed Tennessee and Catherine's attention. They focused on The Ringmaster as he came through the doorway with Sue by his side, her hair tightly held in his fist as he dragged her through the doorway.

"I've been a lot of things, but I've never been a whore," Tennessee said, then looked over at Catherine. "You ever been a whore?"

Catherine slammed her baseball bat into her open palm and shook her head with a smile. "Nope. Papa ain't raise no whores in his house."

The Ringmaster laughed as he pulled Sue's hair so hard her body slammed into the floor at his feet.

"Comedians! Sweet, pretty, little fucking comedians. That's good," he said.

Letting go of Sue's hair, The Ringmaster quickly slammed his foot into the middle of her back, pinning her down. He leaned forward to place his weight on her.

"It's real good because I enjoy a laugh as much as the next guy." The Ringmaster smiled as he his words continued, "So, tell me jokers, have you ever heard the one about the four whores in the whore house?"

The Ringmasters eyes moved from Catherine to Tennessee; his face looked shocked as his gaze slowly danced between them, his hand covering his cartoonish lips as he looked down at Sue. "Your friends have never heard the joke about the four whores in the whore house! Can you believe that, blondie?" The Ringmaster laughed and slapped his hand onto his knee. Sue felt the bones of her rib cage press harder and harder into the wooden floor.

Sue's head turned toward Catherine. Catherine could see

the blood on the girl's face, mixed with tears that came falling from her eyes as that large boot pushed down onto her. Sue was trying to say something. She was trying to push out words, but the pain wasn't letting her. She just put her hand out to Catherine and softly mouthed her request. It was a sight that sent a chill through Catherine's body, to know that she didn't even have the strength to speak much less fight. To know that Sue was so broken all she could do was mouth *Help me.*

Catherine placed both her hands around the handle of the bat, taking a quick step forward. The Ringmaster raised a finger and slowly started waving it back and forth.

"No, no, no," he said softly as his right hand went to his back and quickly reappeared with a loaded revolver pointed down at Sue. "Not so fast, honey. We're just getting ready to start the party!"

Catherine stood still, staring at The Ringmaster. He pulled back the hammer of his gun. A chilling red smile grew on The Ringmaster's face, screaming 'Game over! You lost!'

Catherine was waiting for that sound, the sound of the bullet racing through the air to find its soft target. She wondered if she could get a swing off before that sound, or maybe one after. It was a wicked thought, one that Catherine hated herself for even letting cross her mind, but it was true. Once that gun fired, she would have an opening, a small one, but an opening, nonetheless.

But the chilling sound never came. There was no bullet flying through the air, just a body. A third person came leaping through the doorway, landing on the back of The Ringmaster. The two men flew over the railing and landed on the staircase below. As painful and shocking as the sound of their bodies hitting those steps was, it didn't slow them down. They were both on their feet, taking shots at one another. It was like an unruly bar room brawl with The Ringmaster taking jabs into Adam's ribs. Adam plummeted down the stairs and landed at

Faith's feet. The Ringmaster smiled as he slowly started walking down the steps.

His eyes met Faith's as he said, "Oh, look what we have here." He let out soft laugh until his eyes fully focused on Faith, who stood in the darkness. She was shaking, but even with her hands moving around in the darkness, he could still make out the barrel of the gun.

The Ringmaster stopped moving and put his hand up slowly. "Hold on now, sweetie. You're gonna wanna be real careful with that."

Faith took a step forward with the gun in her hands. From the top of the steps, she heard Tennessee scream.

"Shoot the mother fucker, Faith!"

The Ringmaster's head turned back. "Shut the hell up!" he hissed out, but before he turned back around, he smiled at Catherine and Tennessee. The duo looked at one another then back at The Ringmaster's shit-eating grin

"The fuck is he smiling about?" Tennessee asked.

Catherine shrugged. "No ide—" Before she could finish her statement, Catherine felt her body go flying toward the floor.

When her chest slammed into the wooden floor, she felt a large breath of air push out of her lungs. Just like that, she was winded and out of every bit of energy she came into the house with. She slowly rolled over to see what it was that knocked the wind out of her, but when she got onto her back, all she saw was Tennessee's legs kicking in the air as Daniel stood tall with both his hands around her neck.

"You stupid little bitch!" Daniel screamed into Tennessee's face.

Catherine's hand went to her side in hopes of grabbing hold of her bat, but as her fingers brushed the hardwood she could hear the knocking and banging as it cascaded down the staircase. It rolled quickly down to the feet of The Ringmaster as if he called out to it. He still had his hand up looking at his older brother, then The Ringmaster's head slowly turned toward Faith.

"Well, it looks like we're at a bit of a standoff, aren't we?" The Ringmaster said as he leaned over to pick up the bat.

"Don't, don't do that," Faith said weakly.

The Ringmaster stood back up with the bat in his hand. "You've got the gun and my big brother, well..." The Ringmaster's head turned backward once again to see Tennessee's legs as they dangled in the air, then he smiled, looking back at Faith. "He's got his hands full. So how about you just put down the gun?" The Ringmaster said as he rested the bat along his shoulder, taking one slow step down the stairs.

"Stop that!" Faith screamed.

The Ringmaster laughed. "Stop what?" he asked.

"Shoot..."

"Him." Soft, broken words could be heard coming from Tennessee's slightly blue lips as she clawed at Daniel's hands. Tennessee's nails tore into his skin, but the giant stood there squeezing with everything he had.

Faith's eyes jumped from Tennessee to The Ringmaster. She didn't know what to do. She was scared and worried, but most of all, she was mad. Not mad that she was sold and held like some pig being harvested for dinner, although that thought did piss Faith off royally. What she was mostly mad about was that this was all left up to her. Like some sick cosmic joke, the universe decided she was the best choice to end the madness and save them all.

"Let her go!" Faith screamed.

The Ringmaster took another step forward, and as he did, Faith took a step back. "Put the gun down," he said gently.

Faith shook her head. "Don't come any closer, I'm warning you." Her voice wasn't as strong as The Ringmaster's; it was shaky and a bit uncertain.

This all just made The Ringmaster smile as he continued to

walk down the steps saying, "What are you gonna do, shoot me?" But before he could part his lips to let out his chilling laugh, a loud blast was heard, causing Faith to stumble back, trip, and land on her ass by the front door.

It was done. The universe's sick task was done; Faith finally pulled the trigger. She rested her head on the door with her eyes closed. Faith could hear the zombies outside moaning and clawing into the wood of the house. It wouldn't be long before they were inside moaning and clawing at them. Faith's eyes shot open as she heard a slow clap fill up the room.

The Ringmaster clapped ever so slowly with the bat tucked under his left arm. "Well, I'm impressed!" The Ringmaster said as he leaned down to look at the bullet hole in the step below him. "Had I been a midget or a fucking ant, you might have gotten me." He laughed as he grabbed the handle of the baseball bat once again and calmly made his way down the steps.

"No," Faith said softly.

"Honestly, I was scared for a minute. I almost started praying, but then I thought," The Ringmaster spoke as Faith got to her feet.

She held the gun in her hand, watching the clownish monster make his way down the steps and laughing at her. Faith could see his lips moving, but his words weren't making it through. All that seemed to keep replaying was the laugh. All she could see was him laughing.

"I'll leave God out of this, just in case he's not too pleased with me. I don't want him..." The Ringmasters stopped once again as Faith raised the gun. "Not this again. You need me to paint a bullseye on my chest for you?" The Ringmaster's words were followed by an echoing laugh that took over the darkness of the room.

Faith's face turned red, which only amplified the tears that fell from her eyes now. She pulled her finger back, but all she heard this time was a click. She continued to walk forward, pulling back the hammer and pulling the trigger once again, but all she heard was another click.

The Ringmaster laughed and shook his head as he pointed the bat at her. "Looks like you're out of—"

Before he could finish his words, Faith screamed and ran toward the clown. She tossed the gun, causing The Ringmaster to duck to the side as it zipped past his head. When he came up, Faith wailed on him with her fists. She was fighting. For the first time in her life, she was fighting, but it wasn't against some clowns or zombies. At that moment, every swing, every well-landed balled up fist was aimed at her father, and every tear and scream was meant for her husband.

Faith's fist slammed into the jaw of The Ringmaster, and the crazed clown fired back with a backhanded fist of his own that sent Faith down the last two steps. Yet, instead of taking the pain and balling up like Faith was so used to, she grabbed the clown and wrapped her arms around him. Faith's red hair took over the white face of The Ringmaster.

"What the fuck!" The Ringmaster shouted, then he screamed. The Ringmaster swung his body left to right, but Faith's arms and legs were wrapped firmly around him, making it hard for him to pull her off.

Daniel's head popped to the side to see what was going on, which gave Catherine the moment she needed. She shot forward, doing a small roll, and landed at Daniel's feet where she pulled the throwing knife out of his boot. Daniel screamed along with his brother, both clowns filling up the darkness with their howls of pain. The event sounded like a dinner bell to the zombies outside as they pounded harder onto the walls of the farmhouse. Daniel dropped Tennessee to the ground, but Catherine still jammed the knife into his thigh. She twisted and pulled it down, ripping open the whole inner half of his thigh.

The large man dropped to the ground screaming, "You bitch! You fucking bitch!"

Daniel frantically tried to stop the blood from spilling out. The blood was filling up the floor at the top of the staircase. Tennessee rubbed her throat as she watched the pool of blood quickly making its way toward her knees.

"Tennessee!" Catherine shouted, but Tennessee's eyes didn't move from the blood as she watched it overtake her acid washed blue jeans. "Tennessee!" Catherine shouted once again as she pulled at her.

Tennessee turned her head toward Catherine, her eyes glazed over. Catherine wasn't sure if she was in shock or if she was closer to death than Catherine had thought, but Catherine knelt down beside her.

"You need to get Sue." The duo looked over at Sue, who was still passed out and bleeding on the floor.

Catherine looked back down the steps at Faith, who was lying on the floor now, and at The Ringmaster, who was on his knees and holding his face.

"I'm gonna deal with that piece of shit," Catherine said.

She got to her feet and ran down the steps. She picked up the baseball bat as she ran past The Ringmaster.

Catherine got down to her knees and ran her hand over Faith's red hair. "You alright, sweetie?" she asked, and Faith slowly started to sit up.

She spit out dark red liquid that pooled on the floor. Catherine watched as the blood slowly filled up the gap between Faith's feet, then she saw a large bit of white meat fall into the pool, making a splash. Catherine looked at it for a moment then back up at Faith's blood-covered mouth.

Before the two could say anything, The Ringmaster tackled Faith back down to the floor.

"You little shit! Look what you did to my face!" The Ringmaster screamed as he pinned Faith down. "Look what you did to my face!"

He grabbed her light red hair spread out along the old

wooden floor. He held her hair tightly in his fist and slammed Faith's head into the floor over and over again. Blood rained down onto Faith from the large, jagged wound that was on The Ringmaster's face. It was an island of red in a sea of white makeup.

"Look what you did to my face!" he screamed once again.

Catherine shot to her feet behind The Ringmaster. She swung the bat back, holding it behind her head for a quick moment before sending it forward into the side of The Ringmaster's head. The clown tumbled over to the side, the blood from the side of his head mixing with the blood pushing from the hole where his cheek once was.

The Ringmaster slowly turned his head toward Catherine. He put his hand up and softly let out, "Pleeease."

Catherine took a step forward until she was standing right over The Ringmaster. Staring down into his eyes, Catherine smiled and softly said, "Welcome to the greatest show..." She swung the bat down into his face once again, this time smacking into the bottom front row of his teeth. "On Planet Dead!" she screamed.

The Ringmaster put his hand up and tried to speak, but all that seemed to come out was little gargles.

Catherine leaned down, cupping her hand over her ear as she whispered, "What was that? I can't hear you, sweetie!" She stood up straight and raised an eyebrow. "You want an encore? Well..." She raised the bat over her head and nodded. "I guess you gotta give the fans what they want, right?"

The bat came flying down into the face of The Ringmaster, then it popped back into the air, tossing blood along with it. Then back down it came smashing into his face, his nose crumbled under the pressure. Blood was pouring from The Ringmaster's head. Catherine swung the bat once again, this time cracking his jaw. She swung it again and again. She was filled with energy now, she could have kept swinging forever, but then a hand stopped her.

Catherine's head turned, and she saw Sue standing there. "That's enough," Sue said weakly while leaning on Tennessee. "That's enough."

7

YOUR BROTHER IS DEAD

PLANET DEAD

*B*lood and white makeup covered the floor throughout the old house. Bodies were surrounded by bloody footprints as Catherine stood tall among the madness. Looking down at The Ringmaster's broken face, watching as the blood pushed its way past bone and torn flesh, fighting a battle just to end up part of a large pool of blood on the floor. Looking down at all this, Catherine smiled. Then she spit a mixture of blood and saliva on the clown as she stepped over it. The bat made an echoing sound that would have filled the room if not for the pounding and moaning from outside. Catherine walked over to Faith's hauntingly still body and put her hand on the girl's cheek.

Faith's red hair had been overtaken by an even darker red wave spilling from the back of her head. She was blinking slowly, but her eyelids seemed to be the only thing making an effort to move.

Catherine smiled through the tears that were building in her eyes as she said, "We got him Faith." She took hold of Faith's hand and held it tightly, then looked over her shoulder at Tennessee and Sue. "We got him," Catherine said once again.

"That's beautiful and all. Really it is, I'm sure they'll make a movie about it someday called 'Catherine Briggs! Clown Killer!', but can we get to the more pressing matter at hand?" Tennessee spat the words out like a sharp venom of truth as all the boarded-up windows in the living room continued shaking. They had been so wrapped up with the evil inside the house that they forgot what was waiting outside. "What the hell are we gonna do now?" Tennessee asked.

Catherine stood up and looked around at the windows, the smell of decay starting to take over the air. Catherine ran her hands over her face and tried her best to push past the rotten taste that was forming in the back of her throat.

"We get them out of here. We need that van," she said. Catherine walked over to them and ran her finger through Sue's hair, "You doing alright, kid?" Catherine asked.

Sue did her best to put a smile on. It was weak, broken, and as fake as they came, but it caused Catherine to smile just the same.

"All right, well then hold this," Tennessee said as she tossed Sue into Catherine's arms.

Tennessee walked over to Adam who had been passed out through most of the events that took place that night. Tennessee smiled and swung her open hand across his face, slapping him as hard as she could before shouting, "Rise and shine princess! We got some questions!"

Adam's head shook back and forth, and he shot up till he was sitting on his ass, he looked up to see Tennessee towering over him.

"What? What happened?" he said as he looked around the room.

"That clown knocked the fuck out of you. Judging by the looks of you, it might have been a lack of food and not so much the ass kicking that made you pass out," Tennessee said.

Adam's eyes slowly made their way to Sue and Catherine.

He wanted to ask if Sue was okay, if everything was alright but once his eyes found Faith and the blood, he knew nothing was alright. His gaze started to fall when he saw something, something white in the glow of the moonlight. Behind Sue and Catherine's legs, partly covered in the darkness of the room was his brother, The Ringmaster. Adam started to crawl backwards till his back was against the wall and he used that to slowly lift himself up.

"You killed him," he said looking over at Tennessee.

Tennessee put her hand over her heart and smiled as she said, "Who me?" She laughed and shook her head. "I wish, but that kill goes to Babe Ruth over there," she said as she pointed a thumb over her shoulder at Catherine.

"He didn't need to die! He was messed up in the head, but he couldn't help it." Adam said.

Tennessee laughed, "I don't give two shits about him, you, or the dead giant upstairs. All I wanna know is where's the van?" Tennessee asked with her arms crossed over her chest.

"Giant? Van?" Adam repeated.

Catherine nodded. "Yes, the van that we got into, where is it?" she asked.

Adam shook his head and rested it back on the wall as he said, "It's parked down by the tent, but the engine's shot. It died halfway back after getting you two. We pushed it the rest of the way."

Tennessee rolled her eyes and turned around as she said, "He's useless, I say we kill him."

Sue shook her head and slowly took her arm off of Catherine. "No! He didn't do anything, he tried to help me," she said softly, she started walking slowly toward Tennessee, but stumbled, only for a moment causing Catherine's arms to go out to brace her, "I'm fine." Sue said trying to sound stronger than she looked.

She stood upright again and looked at Adam. His head slowly turned toward the top of the steps where his other brother's body was still bleeding out, sending blood cascading down the staircase. A giant dying in the darkness.

Adam hated himself for crying. He couldn't defend it and he couldn't explain why it happened. Still, the tears slowly started to fill his eyes.

You could hear soft moans coming from Daniel at the top of the stairs, nothing to the level of the moans that surrounded the house. Those sounded like they were ripping through the very walls that held up the house.

Sue's eyes came back to Adam and she said softly, "There's nothing left here now. You can help us, and we can all leave together."

Tennessee's head turned toward Catherine and Catherine nodded, causing Tennessee to throw her hands up in the air shouting, "Whatever!"

Tennessee stormed up to Adam, pushing Sue to the side. The girl stumbled but braced herself with the nearby wall. Tennessee and Adam were eye to eye, Tennessee spoke her words slowly like she was talking to a child.

"We need a ride out of this shit hole, but before that, we need some weapons. Where are they?"

Adam mutely stared at Tennessee, the woman's eyes were cold and steely. They made him feel uneasy, which was rare feeling, something only created by his brothers. Yet, in this moment even with living with psychotic cannibals on a daily basis, Adam felt afraid. So, he decided to leave out the bag of guns they had collected over their travels out of his reply.

Adam leaned his head to the side, looking at Sue he said, "Whatever weapons we have, are outside in the shed and as for a ride." He looked down closing his eyes for a moment debating whether or not he wanted to tell them he could fix the van.

Adam looked over at Tennessee's grin and decided he would leave out that fact as well, before looking back up at Tennessee. "There's a truck on the other side of the tent. I don't know if it runs. We never needed to use it. It was too small, we used the van to get everything we needed." The moment the words lift his lips Adam regretted them.

Tennessee shoved Adam back into the wall. "I bet you did get everything you needed. How many times did you need a little sugar, huh shitbag!" she screamed.

Sue leaped toward Tennessee grabbing her arm. "Leave him alone," she said

Adam screamed back, "I didn't mean it like that!"

Tennessee pull her arm out of Sue's grasp causing the girl to fall forward into Adam's arms. Tennessee's finger shot out toward Sue, who was wrapped in Adam's arms.

Tennessee softly said, "Let me give you some advice. Not everyone is your friend. There isn't gonna be someone to come save you all the fucking time." Tennessee started walking closer to the two of them, she looked at Adam then looked over into Sue's weak eyes as she continued, "One day you'll realize no matter how big the world is, no matter how many people smile your way, they're always gonna let you down, and you're always gonna be alone."

The two of them stared at each other for what felt like forever, there was no sound, the moaning outside was still going on, but between the two of them it was just those words hanging in the air until they heard Catherine shout out, "Tennessee!"

Tennessee's head slowly turned toward Catherine keeping Sue and Adam in her peripheral view. "What?" Tennessee sharply let out.

Catherine was now holding her baseball bat firmly in her right hand, she pointed the bat at the door, "Get the damn door! We're going to the shed," Catherine said.

Tennessee looked back at Sue and Adam, she leaned forward and grabbed a handful of Adam's shirt, the young man pulled back slapping her hand away.

"What the fuck? I don't know anything else." he screamed.

Tennessee smiled, "I know that, but if we're going out there, best believe your bitch ass is going out there too," she said.

Catherine started walking toward the door, "Sue watch over Faith, make sure she's ready to move when we get back."

Sue broke free of Adam's arms and slowly made her way toward Catherine, "You're just gonna leave me here?" she asked

Catherine turned her head back to look at Sue. Catherine saw the tears in Sue's eyes and Catherine smiled.

"Sue, if I was just gonna leave you, I wouldn't have come in the first place. I'll be right back, you're in no condition to pull this off." Catherine looked over at Tennessee and then Adam, "No bullshitting, if you can't do it, stay your ass back here," she said as she turned to the door.

Tennessee looked over at Adam and softly whispered into his ear, "She's talking to you Olive Oil."

Adam watched as Tennessee turned and started walking toward the door, he saw her get ready to open the door for Catherine who was braced by the doorway with her bat held tightly.

"Bitch," Adam said softly to himself, his eyes went over to Sue who was standing there looking at the door. He walked up to Sue and stood next to her for a moment before saying, "I'm sorry."

Sue's head turned toward Adam, she stared at him and then looked back at Catherine who was standing there waiting for the war to start.

"I know" She finally said. Adam nodded walking toward the door.

Adam stood by Tennessee, and watched as Catherine put up three fingers, "When you open the door, I'll try to make the best path that I can but you two need to get to that shed," she said, the pair nodded and one of her fingers went down.

Adam closed his eyes for a moment, his life had been turned upside down in the space of a few months. He went from private schools, and small talks at family dinners to kidnapping and hurting people he didn't even know. Adam wished he could say they did it cause they had to, that there was no other choice, that this was the only form of food they had, but he knew the truth. His brothers did it because they liked it and Adam did it because he was scared. Adam eyes opened and he realized he was just as scared now as he was dealing with his brothers.

"I don't know if I can do this," he whispered.

Catherine put down another finger and looked over at Adam, "Then go help—"

She was about to tell him he could stay and help Sue. That she didn't blame him, but none of those words came out. Nothing could be said, her time was stolen from her as Tennessee swung the door open and two of the monsters came crashing through. Their jaws were frantically snapping at Catherine, who had jumped back. The zombies were lying in the doorway as Catherine swung the bat down with all the force she could muster up, cracking open the skull of one of the zombies.

Adam was already stomping on the head of the other and Tennessee was down the front steps racing toward the shed around the corner of the house.

"Bitch," Catherine said softly to herself and then she quickly took off behind her. "Move the bodies and close the door!" she yelled back at Adam.

She was in the middle of the yard with her bat tightly held in both hands, "Bring it on you dead mother fuckers!" she screamed out into the night sky.

This caused the infected to slowly start to turn toward Catherine. First it was just one, then four, but, as she continued to scream into the air, backing up down the hillside, she noticed all of them were turning her way.

It was close to twenty or so, all from different walks of life, she did her best to focus on that, more than the fear. Quickly naming each in her head to take any hidden remorse out of the picture, she swung for their ripe heads.

She watched as a scantily clad woman with a large sword sticking out of her mouth came walking toward her. How the woman planned on taking a bite out of anyone with that in her mouth was beyond Catherine's comprehension, but she became Esmeralda. The whoring showgirl from Brazil who was after the bearded lady's husband.

"Bad Esmeralda!" Catherine said as her bat went flying from her left side to her right, smashing into Esmeralda's neck, causing her to fall to the ground and start rolling down the hillside.

The next two she focused on seemed to be a couple; they were dressed far more formally than Esmeralda was. The man had a button up blue dress shirt, well it used to be blue, now it was whatever dark color blood and blue produced. Catherine followed the bloodstain up to a large hole between his neck and his shoulder; from that hole hung a chunk of flesh that sent a stream of blood down the man's shirt that blended in with his red tie.

The woman was no better; there were large gashes all along her face. She reminded Catherine of The Ringmaster before she used his head as a baseball. That thought made her smile; it even pushed a small laugh from her chest as she started looking at the zombies' hands searching for their wedding rings, so she could label them Mr. and Mrs.

However, as she did that, she saw him. A small boy shuffled

alongside the well-dressed couple; he was wearing a matching bright red tie like the man, his father she guessed. Her eyes were fixed on his glazed over grey eyes. The boy moaned and made his way toward her. It didn't seem as if he was fully aware that she was there, unlike the others. Catherine found herself picturing Jordan, holding his hand and walking alongside Robert. They were just three souls trying to live their normal lives and then the world turned it all upside down.

"Jordan," Catherine said softly.

She stood there as the boy slowly turned his head toward her; she could feel his grey eyes locking onto her. Then his slow movements turned into him speeding toward her with his mouth snapping and his bloody hands out. He was missing four fingers and blood was still spraying from his wounds.

Catherine longed to see Jordan again, but not like this. This was a dead boy, and Jordan was very much alive. Catherine knew that, she believed that, she had to. Catherine put her bat up, getting ready for a swing when blood came flying onto her chest, the boy's head tumbling through the night sky and rolling down the hillside. Catherine's eyes followed it as it rolled past Esmeralda who was slowly making her way back up the hill.

Catherine turned to see Tennessee swinging a machete, cutting through the crowd of zombies, one bloody body part at a time. Adam wasn't too far behind as he started chopping and cutting through the crowd with a small hatchet.

Adam took one large low swing, bashing in the kneecap of the father zombie. The zombie went down quickly, but Adam found himself fighting to pull the hatchet out of the bone. He fell to his ass as he finally pulled the hatchet free, but, on second glance, Adam saw the bloody kneecap still stuck to the blade. He had ripped it right out of the zombie's leg.

A cold sweat started dripping down Adam's forehead as he watched the man frantically clawing his way toward him. He started rushing backward as quickly as he could, kicking up dirt each time his feet kicked away from the zombie. Before he knew it, his back had run into Catherine's legs. Adam looked up at Catherine, who looked over at the quickly crawling zombie. She took a large step forward and swung her bat; the wood met with the softened skull of the zombie, cracking it open and causing blood and brain matter to shoot out like a fountain.

The zombie stopped cold from the impact, but only for a moment before he began racing toward them once again. Once again, Catherine swung down with her bat, but this time, the bat caved into the man's head and his body went limp. Catherine looked back down at Adam and put out her hand to help him to his feet.

"You all right?" she asked.

The skinny young man, hands lightly shaking with the hatchet still tightly held by his white-knuckled hand, nodded.

Catherine dusted off his shoulders as she asked, "Where's the truck?"

Just then Tennessee came running toward Adam and she swung her machete at the left side of his head.

Adam dropped down to his knees screaming, "What the fuck!"

Blood started running down the side of Adam's face. He knew that it was over; the time to pay for all his sins had come. Adam knew everything his brothers did was wrong, and that he was just as wrong for not stopping them. He knew there was a place in hell for those that helped the devil do his dirty deeds, which was just what he did for his brothers.

He tied those girls up...

He dragged the bodies in and out that tent.

Dead or alive...

Screaming or crying...

He did it all.

Adam might have hated himself for it every night, he might

have refused food from time to time, but hate and pain weren't going to bring those girls back. So, as the blood started running down his face and onto his dirty white shoes, he was at an odd peace because he knew he deserved it.

"Hey, you're all right kid. Get up." Catherine's calm voice broke through all of Adam's thoughts of sin and hell.

He looked up at her through the drips of blood that had clung to his eyebrows. Adam's head turned toward Tennessee, who was standing over him with the machete resting on her shoulder, smiling. Adam stood up and slowly turned around to see Esmeralda's headless body lying on the floor behind him. There was blood all around them; drops of it covered Catherine's and Tennessee's faces as they watched Adam come to terms with his new lease on life.

The young man ran his hands over his face trying to clear away the blood, "What the fuck?" he softly said to himself.

Tennessee laughed and was about to spit out a weak apology to Adam, but Sue's blood chilling scream stole everyone's attention.

"Catherine!"

Catherine's head shot back toward the house, the front door wide open. She took off running, swinging her bat, knocking over zombies as she created a path to the house.

"Catherine!" Tennessee screamed out over the moans.

Catherine didn't look back as she shouted out, "Get to the truck!"

She took one giant leap, clearing the stairs to the front porch and, before she knew it, was through the front door staring at the back of a rather large looking man.

Catherine looked past the large shoulders to see Sue backing up slowly, while pulling Faith by her legs, the two were at the bottom of the staircase now, with no place to go but up. With Faith not providing any help, it was gonna be a hard trip.

Sue's eyes burned as the tears started to flow, her chest heaved at the sight of Catherine in the doorway.

"Catherine!" she cried out once again and Catherine swung the bat as hard as she could right into the back of the large man's head.

A loud snapping sound echoed throughout the living room. Catherine hands came back with only half the baseball bat; it had shattered upon impact with the man's skull. Catherine's eyes widened, and her jaw dropped as her gaze went from the shattered bat to the large man. Blood was running down the side of his head, but he never moved.

The man's shoulders rolled for a moment, then his feet shifted as he slowly started to turn around to face Catherine, who dropped what was left of the bat when she saw the large man's face.

"Oh my God," she softly said to herself as she took a step back from the large muscle-enhanced man.

It wasn't his size that shocked Catherine. It was his face, or lack thereof. His mouth was hanging open, with his tongue just swinging ever so freely from one corner of his mouth to the other. There were no lips to hide his large blood -covered teeth as he started slowly walking toward Catherine. His skin seemed to have burned or melted off his face; all that was left was a dark mix of blood and charred skin and these two large bulging grey eyes. There were red veins running throughout them. The man's large muscular arms came out toward Catherine as she took a slow step back, keeping out of reach as the zombie continued moving slowly forward.

"Catherine!"

The man's head quickly turned from left to right, his body seeming to fight between moving forward and turning around toward Sue's scream. Catherine stood there, back against the door frame of the house. She turned to look out the doorway, watching the zombies making their way down the hill after Tennessee and Adam.

Catherine's turned her attention back to the large burnt-faced man; she put her hand out toward the open door, then quickly slammed it shut. The man's head started spinning from side to side once again as his body twisted and turned its way toward the closed door. Catherine started to slowly take side steps, one slow move at a time, till she made her way by one of the many boarded-up windows. Even then, the burnt-faced man was still walking toward the shut door with his hands out.

Catherine's eyebrow went up and then she looked over at Sue who was fighting to get Faith up off the floor. Catherine slowly put her fist up in the air and shook her head. Sue's eyes were fixed on Catherine and then she looked over at the large man, then back at Catherine.

"What the fuck does that mean!" Sue shouted.

As soon as Sue's words hit the air, the massive zombie spun around and started frantically running toward her.

"Oh, shit!" Catherine screamed out as she raced toward the zombie.

She kept her shoulder low and slammed her boots into the floor with every step. The sounds caused the creature to quickly turn, but it turned right into Catherine and her rushing shoulder. Both of them went toppling over onto the floor.

Sue stood up as she watched Catherine trying her best to break free from the massive zombie's grip. His arms were locked around her like a vice grip. Catherine kept her hands pressed up under the zombie's bloody jaw to avoid the jagged teeth that were trying to make their way toward her flesh. Catherine's hands started slipping, sliding off of the blood and slimy flesh he called a jaw inch by inch. With every slip, his head kept getting closer and closer to her.

"Sue!" Catherine screamed out.

Catherine was chest to chest with the monster, so she had

no idea that Sue was already on the case. Sue had run up the stairs when Catherine shouldered the zombie and came back down with the knife that was once buried Daniel's leg. Sue stood over the two, letting Catherine and the monster battle it out between her legs for a moment.

"Hey!" Sue shouted.

Catherine's head shot up and the monster's head snapped up as well, just in time for Sue to drive the knife down into his bulging eye socket.

"Night, night, motherfucker!" Sue said as she twisted the knife left and right.

The muscular arms fell to the side and Catherine started pushing herself away from zombie.

She sat there on the floor for a moment, then looked over at Sue, "What the fuck?!" Catherine yelled.

Sue looked away from the man's face, raising her eyebrow. "What?" she asked.

"I was telling you to stop what you were doing, and listen up," Catherine said as she started getting up off the floor.

Sue rolled her eyes, "I don't speak G.I Joe," she said.

Catherine walked over to the body and stood there looking at him.

"He was odd." Sue said.

Catherine nodded. "He was blind." she replied.

Sue looked over at Catherine and then back at the body, "Well, that could have been way easier than, huh?" she asked. Catherine ran her hands over her face as she walked over to Faith.

"I'm sorry!" Sue shouted out.

Catherine started laughing as she said, "You're always sorry!"

The two women went about getting Faith up without any other words. They slowly made their way through the blood-covered living room, stepping over the blind monster whose head was pinned to the floor with the knife. Sue stared at his face as she stepped over; he was frightening even motionless, but she put him down, which was a far cry from where she was just a few days ago. Hell, it was a far cry from just a few hours ago. When they made it to the door Sue's head turned toward the corner of darkness, where The Ringmaster's black boot stuck out into the light of the doorway. Sue stared at it till she felt Catherine tug on Faith, causing Sue to move forward.

What was lying dead in the darkness, that was the real monster. An evil that preyed on the weak when the world was broken. A monster that didn't care about surviving, didn't care about finding a cure or worrying about why all this was happening.

Finding family, or just finding a moment of safety wasn't on his mind; this monster just wanted to bring the world deeper into the darkness and prove everyone was just as wicked as he was. As Sue took one last look at the blood covered room she wondered if he was right. A honk caused both Sue and Catherine's heads to pop up. A white dirty ice cream truck sat by the steps; the back door pushed open and Tennessee hopped out, dusting herself off.

Slowly turning her head toward the women, "You clowns coming?" Tennessee said.

Sue rolled her eyes and they he started walking down the steps with Faith's body, "Clowns? Really?" Sue said.

Tennessee laughed as they walked to the back of the ice cream truck. "What, too soon?"

As they loaded up Faith into the back of truck, Catherine looked around it. There were old ice cream containers and a freezer, two seats up front, and a sleeping bag in the back that they rested Faith on. Catherine hopped out of the back and closed the doors, leaving Sue and Faith inside. Tennessee went toward the driver's side, but before she got to the door Catherine pulled her by the arm.

The women were face to face now, Tennessee smiled and raised an eyebrow as she said, "What? I know it's not the best ride, but beggars can't be choosers you know?"

Catherine's cold stare didn't leave Tennessee, she studied the smiling woman before softly asking, "Where's Adam?"

8

IT WOULD BE NICE IF YOU GOT YOUR STORY STRAIGHT

PLANET DEAD

The ice cream truck tires raced along the blacktop road away from the farmhouse, from the bodies, from it all. They just wanted to put miles between them and the madness that had entered their lives.

Sue had fallen asleep in the back after an hour of verbally battling with Tennessee. The two were going at it over Adam, Sue's skinny protector.

Tennessee said once they got to the truck, Adam started it up, not knowing that there was a zombie in the back. Tennessee said he fought for his life, and that she was fighting to save him, but there was nothing she could do. That's what Tennessee said, but as Catherine's eyes ran along the dusty interior of the truck, she was starting to think what Tennessee says and the truth weren't one and the same. After hours of screaming and questions, it came down to one pure statement that summed up what everyone was feeling.

"You don't believe me, do you?" Tennessee asked.

Catherine's head turned away from the cool air that was blowing past her open window, she looked over at Tennessee for a short moment then back over her shoulder at Sue. "It doesn't matter if I believe you or not. It's over with," Catherine said.

She turned her head back to look at Tennessee, whose eyes were fixed on the road; the headlights hardly worked, and she had to stay focused to make sure she didn't hit a deer or a pack of zombies. The last thing they wanted was to walk in the dead of night with Faith still being out of commission.

"We just need to move forward," Catherine finally finished.

Tennessee laughed softly to herself and tightened her grip on the steering wheel, "You never believe me." she softly said.

Catherine's eyebrow went up, "What do you mean never?" she asked.

Tennessee shouted, "A fucking zombie got him! I don't see why that's so hard for you to believe!"

Catherine closed her eyes and rested her head back on the seat, "Maybe because you made it very clear you wanted him dead and—" Catherine's words were cut off as Tennessee laughed.

"I never said that but let's be honest. He was killing and raping girls long before he decided to help Barbie back there," Tennessee said.

Catherine softly replied, "He said he didn't take part in that."

Tennessee's head spun toward Catherine, "Would that hold up in court? Oh yes, your honor, my brothers raped, slaughtered and ate some chicks, but not me!" Tennessee mockingly said as she pointed a thumb at herself. "No, sir! I just tied them up and moved the bodies."

Catherine's eyes finally opened to look at Tennessee. "There aren't any more courts. Just us and we don't have the right to decide who lives or dies," Catherine said.

Tennessee turned her head back to the road and smiled. "Seemed like you exercised your rights all over The Ringmaster's face back there."

Catherine looked over at the dark road that was ahead of them; she didn't say another word. Part of her knew Tennessee was right; they were all questioning and labeling Tennessee a murderer in their minds, when they all had some kind of blood on their hands.

There was no way of making it out of this world clean, not if you wanted to make it out alive. Catherine could say her kill was justified, that The Ringmaster was a monster, but what made her excuse any more just than Tennessee's.

Catherine looked out the window once again, "Where are we heading?" she asked.

Tennessee looked back at both Sue and Faith; they were passed out by the empty ice cream containers. Her eyes went back to the road and she softly said, "The CDC."

"What the hell is at the CDC?" Catherine asked.

Tennessee shrugged her shoulders without really looking at Catherine as she said, "That's what Faith's plan was before we met. She's not the brightest bulb in the house, but it sounded as good of a plan as any. Faith and her husband were really big into horror movies and shit. Faith said that the CDC planned for something like this, like if a zombie outbreak ever happened. So, it's the best place to go."

Catherine's head turned toward the window again. "Yeah, well plans change when you get kidnapped. I'm not going on some wild goose chase. I'm going to Savannah."

Tennessee laughed shaking her head as she said, "Nah, Faith wasn't kidnapped. Her husband sold her to The Ringmaster. Told her she was just slowing him down." Tennessee looked over at Catherine's wide eyes. "I know, fucked up, huh?" Tennessee finally added.

Catherine felt bad, but she didn't really care what reasoning Tennessee had behind it all. All that was really running through her mind was how far away from Savannah this road was taking her. She had been through so much to get to her boys; she wasn't ready to just give up.

"It's really fucked up," Catherine softly said, and then let out a long sigh before closing her eyes, "Stop the truck." Catherine said.

Tennessee smiled and turned her head to look at Catherine. "What?" Tennessee asked.

Catherine looked back over her shoulder at Sue who was slowly starting to wake up. Sue jumped in pain as the cuts on her back rubbed up against the cold walls of the truck.

"Stop the truck!" Catherine said once again.

Sue's head turned toward Catherine's voice, then she shook her head and softly mouthed 'No.' unable to let her voice find the word. The truck slowed down and then came to a rolling stop, all that could be heard was the rumbling of the engine and the distant moans throughout the night.

Catherine gazed back at Sue for a moment. Sue sat there staring in disbelief before Catherine looked back at Tennessee.

Catherine softly said, "I have to find my family." Catherine's hand went toward the door and Tennessee's hand shot out onto her shoulder, stopping Catherine from turning away.

"You can't just leave!" Tennessee words came out sharp and cold; for a moment they just hung in the cool night's air, till she followed them up with, "I mean you can't just leave us. Faith and Sue need help, and the CDC is the closest thing I can think of."

Catherine nodded, "I understand that, but I can't go. My boys are in Savannah and I've taken a long enough detour as it is," Catherine said. She put her hands over her face, after everything that had happen tonight, the last thing Catherine wanted to do was this. She looked into Tennessee's eyes and did her best not to look anywhere near Sue and said, "You can handle this. Get them to the CDC. Take care of them."

Sue shook her head once again as her soft voice finally found the word, "No."

Catherine turned to look at Sue, the young broken woman slowly started to move closer toward the front of the truck.

"Let's just go to the CDC first, then we can go to Savannah," Sue said.

Catherine's eyes rested on Sue as she listened to her continue.

"We can rest up. Get a better car, and we'll go non-stop. Right to Robert, Jordan and Peter, I swear." Sue put her hand out and rested it on Catherine's hand. "Please, Catherine."

Catherine looked down at Sue's hand and then quickly pulled hers back. "How do you know about Pete?"

Sue's hand dropped back to her knees, "What?" Sue asked.

Catherine's door pushed open and she jumped out of the truck, slamming the door behind her.

"I said, how do you know about Peter, Sue!" Catherine's voice echoed around the truck and Sue slowly started moving back to the rear doors.

She debated locking it and just telling Tennessee to drive.

There were tears filling up Sue eyes; she was alive because of Catherine. Every moment from this point on was owed to Catherine, a woman who risked her life to save someone she didn't know. Someone who almost got her killed, someone who's been lying to her from the moment they met. Sue stared at the truck's doors through her tear-filled eyes; she owed Catherine and she was finally going to pay her back, with the truth.

"They're not in Savannah!" Sue screamed out.

Quick moving footsteps made their way to the other side of the doors. Sue kept her head lowered to her knees, because she knew what was coming next. She knew that there would be screaming, followed by questions, and maybe even a beating. She knew this would all happen, but the fear of losing

Catherine and being on her own once again was far greater than any other fear Sue had. The back doors of the ice cream truck swung open and the moonlight drilled down on Sue like an interrogation light in an old crime movie. Sue kept her back to the light and to the voice that filled the night with a question she really didn't want to answer.

"How do you know about Peter, Sue?" Catherine asked once again.

Sue kept her back to Catherine as long as she could without answering her, till she felt two hands grab onto her arms. Without any care for the pain that she was already in, Sue was dragged out of the back of the ice cream truck and dropped onto the cool asphalt of the road. She stayed there, taking in the cool feeling that the ground gave, it broke through her pain. Sue was staring up at the moon until Catherine's face came into view and block out the light.

"How do you know about Robert's brother and what do you mean, they're not in Savannah!" Catherine screamed.

Sue slowly started to get to her feet. When she finally did, she looked down at Catherine's hands, they were balled up into two tight fists, waiting for the wrong answer. Sue ran her fingers through her hair before crossing her arms over her chest.

"When I told you about my last night with Sam and Dean, I didn't tell you about the days that lead up to that night," Sue said softly.

Catherine started walking slowly toward her as Sue was slowly backing away. She only got two steps before her ripped and bloody back was pressed up against the metal of the ice cream truck's open door. Catherine kept moving forward till she was eye to eye with Sue.

"Well, tell me now. And no lying, Sue. Tonight's not a good night for lying," Catherine said.

Sue nodded and swallowed deeply before starting again, "We were holding up in our house, like everyone else in the complex. Like Peter and his mom used to," Sue said. She went to ease her back off the metal door, only to have Catherine push her back into place. Sue closed her eyes, "We were all just trying to look out for ourselves; the thought of helping anyone else didn't even come into my mind until they showed up."

Catherine softly said, "Until who showed up?"

Sue stared into Catherine's eyes. The woman wanted to strangle Sue, tie her to the back of that truck, and drag her ass down to Savannah. That's what her mind wanted to do, but as she stared into Sue's eyes, the last eyes to have seen her boys, all Catherine could do was silently cry.

"A few weeks after the outbreak someone kept coming by and knocking on our door. Every day at 8 a.m. like clockwork, asking if anyone was home. I think he was doing it for everyone," Sue said.

Sue's eyes looked back into the truck; Faith was still passed out on the sleeping bag and Tennessee was sitting there, with her hands on the steering wheel and her eyes on Catherine and Sue through the rear-view mirror.

"We didn't answer the first few times, but then the Internet went out and the radio. Cell phones were down for a month by then. We lost all connection to the outside world, so when we heard that knock, we rushed to the door, just to see another person." Sue stopped her story; she hung her head and started to cry out, "I'm sorry, I'm so sorry."

Catherine's hand went on Sue's cheek and she lifted the girl's head, till they were eye to eye again, "Finish the story." The soft words sent a chill through Sue's body.

She didn't want to continue, but Sue knew she didn't have a choice, she owed Catherine this much.

"I opened the door and they were just standing there, the man had an awkward smile on this face when he saw us. He looked down at the boy and just said 'You were right' and the boy just kept his eyes on me and nodded and he said 'I know.'

The three of us just stood there looking at one another for what felt like forever before Dean and Samantha came to the doorway. We had some small talk or what passed for small talk back then. He wanted us to pull together and help one another. Dean was so grateful to have another guy around that he jumped at the idea of helping." she said.

Sue smiled as she thought back on the moment and then was pulled back to reality when she felt Catherine's finger flick her in the forehead.

"Is there something funny?" Catherine asked, and Sue shook her head quickly. Catherine nodded as she said, "I thought not. Get to the point! Where the hell are my boys!" Catherine shouted.

Sue jumped, "I don't know! The week before I left a ton of military trucks and people rolled up to our gate," Sue said, she ran her hands over her face and sighed into them before softly saying, "The last time I saw them, they were handcuffed and being loaded up onto a truck. The only reason they didn't get us..." Sue stopped, pulled her gaze up from the floor, and stared into Catherine's eyes as she said, "The only reason they didn't get us was because Jordan told us to hide. He jumped a fence and told us to hide. Jordan saved us." Sue softly finished her story and her eyes dropped back down to the road.

"So, let me see if I got this right." Catherine's hands folded together on the top of her head as she started to pace back and forth slowly. "My boys saved your skinny ass. Helped you and your fuck buddies survive and you repay them by letting them get rounded up like fucking dogs?" Catherine said

Sue shouted, "It wasn't like that!"

"Then what the fuck was it like Sue? You knew what happened to them this whole time and you let me—" Catherine's words were cut off by the sound of Tennessee rolling down the old clunky window.

"Y'all might want to get back in the truck," Tennessee said

softly.

Catherine put up her hand and shouted, "When we're done!"

Tennessee started rolling up her window and rested her head back, "Okay." she softly said to herself.

Catherine's hand came down and her arms folded over her chest, then her arms dropped, and she softly said, "Sue," like a soft whisper she didn't want the world to here.

Sue's face was buried in her hands. She wanted so bad for the ground to open up and shallow her. Catherine was right; everyone was always risking their lives to save her and all she ever did was run and let them down.

"I was too scared. Sam and Dean were dead. I was alone." Sue's head came up and she shouted, "I'm sorry, Catherine!"

When her eyes started to focus through the tears, Sue could see the fear in Catherine's face. Catherine slowly took a step back. Sue went to turn around, but Catherine grabbed Sue's hand and started pulling her.

Catherine screamed, "Don't turn around, just get in the fucking truck!"

The two women jumped into the back of the ice cream truck and heard the motor start up.

"I told you to get back in the truck," Tennessee's voice sung over the rattling of the engine.

Catherine's head spun around, "Just Drive!" she hollered.

Sue wasn't focused on them; her eyes were focused on the figures that were slowly making their way out of the darkness of the woods. She watched as the dead slowly made their way from beyond the trees; first there were three, then seven, then twenty, then there were too many to count. All of them were making their way toward the light in the back of the ice cream truck.

Sue was on all fours, her hands lightly resting on the metal of the truck, so she wasn't ready when the truck took off. No one was. Catherine's body slammed into the broken freezer that once held summer treats for the joyful little children. Then she shot forward into the glass window with the color ice cream sticker. Her head smashed into the glass and her body dropped down next to Faith.

"Catherine!" Sue screamed and crawled over to her.

Catherine was out cold, and the truck was racing down the road. Sue held Catherine's head in her lap and stared at the blood that was covering the back of the truck. There was nothing joyful about this world and as Sue looked down at the gash on Catherine's head, she wondered if there ever would be joy again.

Sue's thoughts stopped as a zombie leapt through the air, his upper body slapping into the metal of the truck's floor. His dark black hair blew in the wind as he started clawing at the cool metal of the truck.

"Umm, Barbie, you mind handling that," Tennessee shouted out from behind the wheel.

Sue stared as the zombie's body was dragged along the road, slowly starting to come undone. First, his feet, and then his knees. Instead of making it more difficult for it to get in, all this was making it easier for him to pull himself up into the back of the truck.

Sue sat there, part of her wanted him to make it, and part of her wanted him to kill her. She didn't want to continue on fighting and hiding just to make it to another day. Yet, fate seemed to always be smiling down on Sue.

First with her narrow escape, then with meeting Catherine, and now fate stepped in once again as the door came flying closed, cutting off the zombie's arms and causing him to smack into the asphalt.

Sue watched as his bloodied and broken body rolled into the darkness, and then, with a small kick, sent his arm flailing into the dead of the night as well.

As Tennessee started to gain speed, Sue couldn't see anything but the glow of their taillights, "I think you lost them," Sue said softly.

Tennessee looked back through her mirror and screamed, "Motherfuckers!" She placed her eyes back on the road and softly said, "She dead?"

"*N*o!" Sue shouted, she looked down at Catherine for a moment then said "I mean, I don't think so. She hit her head pretty bad." Tears slowly started to fall down her cheeks. "Don't be dead," she softly said.

Tennessee's head turned back trying to get a better look. "Nah, that's just a nasty cut. Blood doesn't always mean danger," Tennessee said.

"How can you be sure?" Sue asked.

Tennessee's head turned back toward the road and she let out a laugh. "I'm not sure, but I used to have a roommate that would slice her head up. She said it gives you the most blood with the least pain."

Sue's head spun around. "Why the hell did she do that?" Sue asked.

"She was odd, always doing shit for one crazy plan or another. Some people are always trying to plan out life." Tennessee's head turned to look at Sue. "You look like a planner."

"You don't know me," Sue said.

"Nope. I guess Mrs. Briggs and I got that in common," Tennessee said as her eyes went back to the road. "We don't know you at all, blondie."

Sue's eyes slowly fell onto a blood-covered Catherine; she ran her hand over Catherine's hair. "It's gonna be okay," she said. Sue's eyes closed to hold back the tears that were forming. "We're gonna be okay."

9

REMEMBER THAT?

PLANET DEAD

"Tiffany...Tiffany."

Jordan's lips were parting ever so slowly as he looked up at his mother and father.

Catherine laughed, holding onto Robert's hand tightly. Her next words came out soft with a dash of concern.

"What's he talking about? Who's Tiffany?" Catherine asked.

Staring down at Jordan's rich brown skin, Catherine got lost in the sight of her son. His shaggy, wild hair reminded her of his constant refusal to get a haircut.

Reminded...

The word rolled over and over in Catherine's mind. She put her free hand out and rested it on his dark little fro and softly said once again, "Who's Tiffany, baby?"

Reminded?

Jordan stared at her, the empty look in his eyes causing Catherine to pull her hand back as she asked once again. This time the concern wasn't hidden, it was very much leading the way of her question, "Jordan, who's Tiffany?"

Reminded...No, that's not it.

Jordan stood still. His eyes didn't blink; his chest didn't rise or fall. Catherine found herself wondering if he was even alive at all. That thought worried her so much that she found her hand slowly reaching out toward Jordan once again.

"What's wrong with you swee—" Catherine's words died off quickly as a dark leathery brown hand shot out and grabbed her arm. Her eyes quickly ran up the path of the arm till she saw him; his eyes were grey, his skin was cracked and sunken in, but what chilled Catherine's spine was the blood pushing past a set of jagged white teeth running down his jaw.

"Robert?" Catherine asked.

She tried to pull her hand back, but that motion only aggravated the monster. It stepped forward and Catherine went to take a step back, only to feel her other arm pulled forward; her eyes went over to her right to see Jordan, with the same jagged bloody teeth and tight leather skin.

"No."

The word came out softly, but as she felt her skin tighten and rupture under the points of Robert's teeth, her whisper became a blood chilling cry.

"No!"

She was pinned to the floor now. In her mind she knew this couldn't be real; she prayed it wasn't real.

Jordan's head shot forward till he was eye to eye with his mother; his bloody lips slowly parted, causing little drops of blood to fall onto Catherine's eyes. She could feel the horrific shower mixing with her hazel pools as she stared at Jordan. His lips parted and the blood quickly started running down his jaw as he smiled; her boy leaned in closer and screeched, "Remember Tiffany!"

Catherine put her hands up to push her son off, but the boy shot forward, his teeth digging into her neck. Then came the blood.

Not Reminded...Remember...Remember Tiffany?

Catherine's body shot up. She turned to her left and then

her right, but there was no sign of her zombie family. All she could see was the cool metal of the ice cream truck, and the bright yellow glow of the morning sun pushing through the windshield of the truck.

Catherine was breathing fast and heavy; her heart was bashing into her chest. She placed her hands over her face in an attempt to bring her mind back to the real world and away from that nightmare. The tips of her fingers ran over a thin cloth.

"Fuck." Catherine's forehead was delicate to the touch and neatly dressed with gauze and tape. The warmth of the sunlight covered her as she tried to remember what happened the night before, but all she could recall was that dream; all she could remember was...

"Tiffany," a soft voice called out.

Catherine's hands dropped, and she looked around for a moment. It was the same name, still haunting her even while awake. The voice was so weak and faint that Catherine wondered if she was going crazy, if it was coming from inside her head.

Then she looked behind her, laying in a bloodstained corner of the truck was Faith. Catherine crawled over toward Faith. The girl's eyes were still shut, but her lips were quivering ever so lightly. Catherine heard something softly pass her lips. Catherine leaned over Faith and placed her hand on the girl's cheek. "What is it, sweetie?" she asked.

Faith's lips parted, and the name filled up the warm metal truck. "Tiffany."

Looking down at Faith, it became clear that Faith's voice had broken into Catherine's nightmare with that name. Catherine leaned back over Faith again and softly asked, "Who's Tiffany?"

Faith's lips weren't moving anymore; she was still. Faith was so still that she could have passed for dead if it wasn't for the light rise and fall of her chest.

Catherine sat there on her knees looking at the redhead. She had clean white bandages wrapped around her head. Catherine sat there and her mind pulled together the events of last night; she looked down at Faith and wondered how someone or anyone could sell her to those animals, much less her own husband. There was more to Faith than Catherine would ever know. Catherine was starting to realize, no one really knew anyone in this world of the dead.

"Stop moving!" Tennessee shouted.

"It hurts!" Sue replied.

Catherine's head turned toward the window of the truck; she dusted off her knees and slowly started to get to her feet. Stumbling for a moment, Catherine put her hands out to brace herself.

"You make me poke myself one more fucking time Barbie and I swear I'll pour salt on you," Tennessee said.

Sue softly replied, "I'm sorry."

The door to the truck flung open and Catherine's boots smacked into the blacktop of parking lot as she leaped down from the truck. "You little shit!" Catherine said as she started rushing toward Sue and Tennessee.

Sue shot up and started leaping backwards with her hands up, "Catherine, let's talk about this!"

"Talk!" Catherine screamed, her hand went to her head and she closed her eyes. "You wanna talk!" she continued.

Tennessee stood up and started dusting off her jeans. "Lesbians," she said soft as watched Sue and Catherine play their cat and mouse game.

"You wanna talk?" Catherine asked once again.

"Yes, just let me explain," Sue replied.

Catherine closed her eyes as she started to take slow steps

toward Sue. "Go ahead Sue, explain to me. How you left my family to die," she said. Catherine's eyes opened, and she pointed at Sue. "Explain to me why you've been lying ever since I laid eyes on your little blonde ass!" Catherine shouted. She took another step forward and Sue tumbled over something landing on her back.

She let out a scream. When Sue's eyes came up, she saw Catherine was frozen, just staring off into the distance. Sue slowly started to sit up and when she did, she saw what stopped her weak attempt at an escape. Bloody tan boots laid under Sue's legs; she started scrambling to her feet, walking backwards from the dead soldier lying in the summer heat.

His organs had been ripped from his body and scattered all around him. Yet, it was his face that got to Sue the most, his bug-eyed look of terror was trying to burn a place into her memories, she knew she would see his silent scream at some point in her future nightmares. Sue kept backing up until she bumped into Catherine, who was still staring off into the distance of the parking lot.

"This is the CDC?" Catherine asked softly.

"Yeah," Tennessee said as she folded her arms over her chest, her black jacket tightened around her. The summer heat was strong, but she still refused to remove the jacket even though Sue had asked many times. The final time Sue asked, Tennessee had thrown the first aid kit at her, and told her to make herself useful.

"This was our last great hope? Our only good plan?" Catherine asked as she walked over to the pool of blood and leaned down; her fingers dipped into the dark red and came back up with a metal tag, attached to a chain around the soldier's neck.

She ran her thumb over the raised metal and looked over at Tennessee and Sue. "Private Valdez, doesn't seem to agree with you girls," Catherine said and then looked back into the distance and laughed. "I don't think they agree with you two either."

The city had fallen apart a few months ago. No one knew what this was; no one knew how to fight it. Fingers were pointed, plans were made, but, in the end, people died. One way or another, people died. The parking lot was littered with tanks, overturned cars. Beyond all that was a large fence with razor wire wrapped around the top; beyond the fence was a hoard of moaning mindless zombies. The gate shook with each body that stumbled into it.

"What's the plan? You two gonna ask them nicely to step aside?" Catherine laughed and pointed at Sue. "This is your show, Sue! What's next?"

"Listen, I understand you're upset," Sue softly said as she started to walk over to Catherine. By the time she leaped over, Catherine was already standing, staring at her. Sue stood there, looking into Catherine's eyes as she said, "but you don't have to be a bitch about it! This was a solid plan."

Catherine smiled. "This was a shit-show, not a plan. You two rolled the dice and look what we got!" Catherine turned around to look back at the CDC, "A greeting party of zombies, a shit load of problems, and an even bigger bag of lies." She looked over her shoulder at Sue and softly said, "But not a plan in sight."

Tennessee raised her hand. "Actually, I have a plan." Catherine and Sue's heads both turned as Tennessee continued ."A pretty good one, but I'll just wait till this little lover's spat is over with."

Catherine and Sue weren't best friends; they didn't know each other's birthdays, nor did they have late night talks about the future. They didn't have history, but they did have trust. Sue knew deep down inside, that she was the reason their newly formed bond was now broken. While Catherine was passed out in the back of the truck, Sue had created many different scenarios of how she was going to explain herself. Each scenario ended the same, with Sue flat on her ass and Catherine being held back from killing her. She couldn't think of a way to make it better, so she just went along with making it worse. Sue looked at Catherine and then rolled her eyes, turning to face Tennessee.

"What's the plan?" Sue asked

Catherine's eyes were locked on the back of Sue's blonde head. Catherine didn't blink, not even as the sun shifted toward her light brown eyes; she simply continued to glare at Sue.

"We open the gate to the fence," Tennessee said with a large smile. Yet, as Catherine and Sue's eyes locked onto Tennessee, her smile started to fade. She could see in their eyes that they didn't get the underlying genius behind her plan of action. Tennessee rolled her eyes and pointed at the Ice Cream truck, "And turn the fucking truck on? To play that jingle," Tennessee said.

Sue laughed and put her hand over her chest, "Oh, thank God. You had me worried for a minute. I thought your whole plan was to open the gate and let the zombies out. But no, your plan is to open the gate, let the zombies out, all while ringing the dinner bell!"

Sue turned around to look at Catherine who was staring right at her. "I'm sorry Catherine. I'm really, really sorry. I'm sorrier than anyone will ever know." Sue's hands came up into a prayer position, "Please, for the love of all that is just, don't let Tennessee get us killed."

Catherine closed her eyes and leaned her head back for a moment. She took a deep breath, followed by another, then her eyes slowly opened looking up at the deep blue sky as the sweat on her light brown skin glistened in the hot sun.

She wanted to beat Sue's face in. To leave her on the ground begging for mercy, only to find none. Catherine wanted her to hurt, but what she wanted didn't matter, not at that moment.

Catherine knew there would be a time and place for her and Sue, but for now she played nice.

"It's a good plan," Catherine said as her head came back down from the sunlight. She looked over at Tennessee and nodded. "It's a good plan."

Tennessee shoved her hands in her pockets and did her best not to look directly into Catherine's eyes as she said, "Thanks." She looked over at Sue and smiled as she spit out, "I told you."

Sue rolled her eyes and then threw her hands up into the air as she started walking back toward the truck. "Whatever! I've had a good run I guess. I didn't get married, didn't get my degree, but I went to Vegas," Sue laughed and spun around with her hands on her hips looking at the two Tennessee and Catherine. "So, I guess I can die a happy woman," Sue said.

She spent the past few months avoiding and running from zombies, and now here she was calling them over for an afternoon chat. It was crazy and desperate, but that's what they were.

There was nothing left. No other choice. They were in the heart of the city. The military failed to protect it; the virus took over Atlanta faster than anyone could have predicted. She knew this was it. They needed to get into that building because there was nowhere else to go.

"We just got to get Faith. She's fading in and out, but the fact that she's up at all is a miracle," Catherine said as she started to walk over toward Private Valdez's weapon. She picked it up and started looking around for the magazine clip, slowly making her way toward the man's body.

"Wait, Faith's awake?" Sue asked and

Catherine nodded. "Yeah, she's slowly coming around. She kept saying Tiffany over and over." Catherine looked at Sue as she added, "Then she passed out."

Sue's eyes quickly went from Catherine to Tennessee. "You know what that's about?" she asked.

Tennessee's shoulders quickly shrugged as she turned to look at the truck. "No, we were prisoners, not sorority sisters," Tennessee said softly as her eyes locked on the window of the truck.

"So, you don't know who Tiffany is?" Sue asked once again.

But Tennessee seemed to be miles away. She was back in that tent, with her hands tied above her head, blood running down the side of her head. Smelling the vodka-filled breath of Happy and listening to The Ringmaster's nightmarish laugh. Tennessee was lost in that moment when she thought her life was over, when she thought there was no hope left, then she heard a soft voice through the darkness say 'leave her alone'.

It was a soft, broken scream that caused Tennessee's head to turn to the side. In that moment, she saw her for the first time. Faith was the only person to speak up for Tennessee. They were in the same hell, yet Faith was willing to risk her life just to help.

"Tennessee!" Catherine shouted out, causing Tennessee to be pulled back to the real world. Tennessee shook her head for a moment and then ran her hands over her face.

"You alright?" Catherine asked softly.

Tennessee nodded slowly, clearing away the water that had built up in her eyes. "Yeah I'm fine. I'm gonna go get her ready, you two open up the gate when I start the music."

Tennessee started walking toward the truck and Catherine grabbed her arm quickly. Tennessee's head turned toward Catherine, who was beaten and worn out like the rest of them. Yet, she stood there with the M4 tightly be held in her hands, and two clips peeking out of her cargo pockets.

"I'm okay," Tennessee said softly. Catherine nodded letting go of her arm.

Catherine looked over at Sue and sighed. "Before we do this, maybe you should change," Catherine said.

Sue's eyes went down to her bloody white tank top and the stained red cutoff jeans that hugged the top of her thighs. "And where am I gonna—" Sue's words cut off as Catherine's head nodded to Valdez's mutilated body. "No. No. No! That's not happening!"

~

Sue stood there in bloodstained camouflage pants and a cut-up tan shirt; her eyes were fixed on Tennessee, who was laughing at Sue's sagging pants.

"I feel like a grave robber," Sue said.

"Better a grave robber than a happy meal," Catherine said with a light smile before turning back to the madness they were about to face. "Let's do this. We'll open the gate when the music starts. It should be enough to draw them out toward the truck."

Catherine looked over her shoulder at Tennessee. "When they get close, start the truck up and take off. Lead them away till you can get back here," she said

Tennessee nodded as she started walking toward the truck. She heard the sound of Catherine's combat boots smacking into the ground and Sue's pitter patter not far behind. Then, Tennessee heard a voice, and it sent a chill over her.

"Tiffany...Tiffany."

The frantic whispers filled Tennessee's head; her thoughts became a spiral of panicked voices. One voice screamed to turn back; it pleaded for a moment of clear thought but was forced back into the shadows by more malevolent voices.

Voices that screamed for justice, revenge, and blood! There

was a small part of Tennessee that wanted to walk away. There was a part of her that wanted to move on, but as her footsteps got closer to the truck, that part of her started to slowly die, much like the rest of the world. Faith's eyes opened to see Tennessee sitting on her chest, hand firmly pressed against Faith's lips.

"Why?" Tennessee hissed out, leaning in slowly and pressing all her weight onto Faith, Tennessee pressed Faith's bandaged head into the metal floor of the truck. The bright white bandage was quickly being taken over by a dark red. "Why fucking now? Huh? Why now, Faith?"

Tears started running down Faith's face and through the blur of her tears, Faith could see Tennessee was crying as well. The two women were crying together, much like they did every night for the past few weeks, but this moment was different. There was no speculation, no guessing, no hope. They knew how this was going to end, as Tennessee let out a long deep sigh. Leaning into Faith's ear, she softly whispered, "I can't let you ruin this."

Faith's chest was rising and falling; Tennessee could feel every fearful beat Faith's heart made. She was trying desperately to fight off Tennessee. Faith was using every little bit of strength she had, but as Tennessee pressed on her head once again, Faith knew she wasn't going to make it out of this alive. Faith closed her eyes tightly, trying to slow the river of tears.

Tennessee's head came up slowly, till she was eye to eye with the girl. She took her free hand and cleared away her own tears, before smiling and wiping Faith's eyes as well.

"Don't do that, don't cry. You're better than that," Tennessee said. She closed her eyes and softly said, "I'm gonna have to kill you, Faith." Faith's eyes opened to see a faint smile on Tennessee's face after those words.

Tennessee rolled her neck till it cracked, then she slowly pulled out a rusty metal hook, with an old wooden handle. As the sunlight shifted, it cause a new set of tears on Faith's face to sparkle. Faith started fighting again, shaking her head back and forth until Tennessee's hold got tighter.

Fingernails started cutting into Faith's cheek. "I told you don't do that! You're better than that damn it!" Tennessee said sharply.

Tennessee's left hand came up, dragging the rusty hook along with it. Green eyes meet brown eyes and, in that moment, they both shared the same thought: this didn't need to happen. The hook came down quickly. Even with all the brown and orange rust, it still slide in smoothly, finding a new home in the side of Faith's neck.

The green eyes went wide, wider than ever before. It wasn't her monster or a father. It wasn't her drunk of a husband. It wasn't even a crazed rapist clown that led to this moment. It was Tiffany. A woman Faith thought of as a friend. Tennessee pulled the hook out, ripping off a chunk of Faith's flesh with it.

"I'm sorry," Tennessee said softly as the hook came down once again, this time finding its way into the middle of Faith's chest.

The girl's head dropped back to the cool metal of the floor, her eyes fixed on the sun outside. She did her best to focus just on that, to try and block out the pain as the hook came down into her repeatedly.

Before Tennessee knew it, Faith was gone. Blood poured from her body and started filling up the old grayish sleeping bag. Tennessee stood up slowly, allowed the wooden handle to slip from her fingers, and listened to the sound of metal on metal as it hit the truck floor.

There was blood everywhere, all over Tennessee's jeans and shirt. Tennessee sat there in a trance as her eyes took in Faith's lifeless body. She felt torn, part of her felt just in killing Faith. Faith was a weak link in the world and Tennessee was sure that in time she would have told Catherine everything, but there was another part...a small little voice in Tennessee's head that was crying for the loss of her only friend.

When the thought of Catherine entered her mind, she spun around. Through the glass window covered with stickers, she could see Sue and Catherine standing by the gate, waiting for the signal. Tennessee ran her hands down her jeans trying her best to clean away the blood, but the red stained her soft white skin. She wiped her eyes with her forearms and then leaned over toward the driver's seat.

With a flick of a switch, that dark moment was overtaken by the joyful melody of the Ice Cream truck. Tennessee got to her feet, stepping over Faith and making her way to the doors.

10

RIGHT BETWEEN THE EYES

PLANET DEAD

*S*ue was fighting past the horde of zombies making their way through the open gate. She pushed and ducked, one corpse after another, until a grayish blood-covered hand swung through the air and grabbed her wrist. Sue started to scream, but, just as fast as the zombie took hold of her, it dropped back to the ground as the butt of Catherine's M4 slammed into the side of its head.

"Keep moving. The music won't keep them—" Before Catherine could finish her thought, the joyful music that filled the air came to a chilling stop. All that could be heard were the moans and the shuffling of bodies along the asphalt. Catherine looked over her shoulder at a sea of dead eyes looking back at her. She swung around with the M4 at the ready and started shuffling backwards.

"Move, Sue," she whispered. The duo slowly trekked along, never taking their eyes off the hoard.

There were many events throughout the past three months that caused Sue to believe she was going to meet her maker: protecting the housing complex from a school bus of zombies, hiding out from the military as they went from house to house rounding up people, and being locked in that trunk by a killer clown, all came to mind. Yet, there was no moment clearer in her head than right now.

"We're gonna die," Sue said softly, as if only to herself, hoping the universe wouldn't overhear.

Catherine shook her head. "No! Just fucking move!"

The first wave of monsters pushed forward and Catherine opened up fire. As the hoard made its way toward them, she was taking whatever shot she could get. Catherine gave Sue no choice in the matter as she backed up quickly, forcing Sue to move or be run over.

The two women made it through the gate, but there was no hope of closing it, no hope for them. Catherine stumbled over a dead body, landing on her back. She was looking up, letting it all wash over her when she heard Sue scream, "Get up!"

Catherine sat up and continued firing at the zombies, but they were closing in on them too fast. Sue grabbed Catherine by the arm, pulling her up to her feet. The two women looked at one another and then back at the sea of the dead as Sue softly said, "We're gonna die."

Catherine's eyes were locked on the zombies; she didn't blink, she didn't look away, because she knew if she did, she wouldn't be able to control the tears that were going to fall as she said, "Yes."

"I'm sorry." Sue's voice was cracking. "I'm sorry for everything."

"You should be," Catherine said as a small smile grew on her face.

Sue smiled as she placed her hand in Catherine's. The women closed their eyes and listened to the moans as they got closer. This was it.

This was the end.

A roar filled the air, then another followed. The heart-stopping sounds pulled the duo from the arms of death and gave them something they had been praying for...

A break.

Catherine's eyes popped open as she watched a zombie's skull explode, its body tumbling to the ground. The scene was quickly playing out before her as zombie after zombie dropped to the ground, Catherine could tell the roar was the sweet sound of gunfire. Another body hit the ground and, before they knew it, bullets and blood painted the sky.

The sound of the rounds firing and the ghoulish moans started to drown out the sound of Catherine's heartbeat. Catherine's M4 went back up and she started firing along with her mystery heroes. That one shot pulled her from the brink of death and tossed her back into the war that was life.

"Keep moving!" Catherine screamed.

Sue took off running. Catherine was right behind her, firing off a few shots every few moments. The shots were quick and loud, but Catherine could hear the screams coming from Sue. "Tennessee! Tennessee!"

Catherine's eyes saw the dark-haired Tennessee fighting her way up the gate. There was razor wire all along the top, but Tennessee didn't seem to care; she was racing for her life. Catherine started releasing fire on the zombies that were trying to make an easy meal out of Tennessee.

Shots filled the air as Tennessee's body tumbled over the gate and landed on the hard ground below. She didn't move for a moment, which caused Sue to take a step forward.

Sue was ready to race to her side, but she felt a hand slam into her chest. "Get inside Sue!"

Sue's head turned toward the voices. When her eyes hit his face, a world of questions were released in her head, but there was no time to ask as the hand grew more forceful, pushing Sue back.

"We can't leave her!" Sue said

Catherine's eyes went toward Tennessee who was slowly rolling to her feet. "Move your ass, Tennessee," she said to herself as she continued to let round after round fly into the massive wave of zombies heading toward them.

Tennessee got to her feet and was slowly moving toward the building when a man ran toward her, grabbing her by her hips and scooping her off the ground. Catherine's eyes followed the two figures as they raced toward the CDC; just like Sue, Catherine's mind was full of questions. The man who held Tennessee had dark brown skin, most likely from the hot summer. He was taller than Catherine, with a lined-up haircut, and shiny black waves that ran all along the top of his head.

His head turned toward Catherine and he smiled that sly smile that she always saw before withdrawing money from the bank.

"Pete?"

Catherine let the name slowly fall from her lips, it couldn't be Pete. What would Robert's brother be doing here? Catherine slowly started to turn around, her heart pounding. It was a simple turn, but it seemed to take forever in that moment. When Catherine's eyes came upon the CDC doors, she saw them: Robert and Jordan firing into the hoard of zombie.

Catherine took in the sight of her husband. He stood tall; his dark skin and sweat shined in the sunlight. His beard had grown out since she last saw him. It was unkempt, with a new river or grey hairs running through the black. There was no fighting this; her tears had finally won the battle as Catherine softly said his name. "Robert."

"Catherine! Run!" Sue shouted, pulling Catherine back into the real world once again.

She started racing toward the building, but the fire was back in her legs. The only thing that seemed to make its way into Catherine's mind was her pain.

Her legs...

Her head...

But when her eyes fell onto Jordan, she swallowed the hurt and kicked into another gear. Running past Robert, Catherine burst through the door.

She almost knocked Jordan over as his arms wrapped around her. He buried his face into Catherine's chest; he was trying to hide the tears that were coming, but she felt them fill up her white tank top. Catherine's hand tussled Jordan's hair and she pulled back to look at him, she stared at the boy.

"Jordan?" she softly asked. It felt like him, looked like him, but part of Catherine still wondered if she died outside and this was all some kind of dream.

The boy smiled through the tears and just softly said, "I knew you were alive!"

Robert and Peter slammed the door shut and a woman in a dirty white lab coat touched a keypad. Two large metal shutters started to lower behind the glass doors.

Robert rushed over to his family. His arms swung around Catherine and for the first time in what felt like forever, Robert ran his fingers through Catherine's hair and kissed her. His family was whole again.

Catherine's eyes were watering as she looked past the gap between Robert's arm; she could see Sue standing there staring at them.

Catherine slowly broke away from her family and moved toward Sue.

Sue softly asked, "You're not gonna kick my ass, are you?"

Catherine smiled and threw her arms around Sue, pulling the girl in for a deep embrace. They both let out a sigh. It was finally over.

"Maybe tomorrow," Catherine said.

Catherine pulled away from Sue and looked over at her husband as she asked, "Wait, what the hell are you doing here?"

Robert shook his head and looked over at Peter, who started

to laugh, messing up Jordan's hair, "It's a long story. I don't think you're ready for it." Robert said.

The Briggs boys started to laugh and while the walls outside were lined with flesh eating zombies, Catherine didn't care. Her eyes washed over Jordan, then Peter, then they landed on the hazel gaze that was Robert's eyes. Catherine knew nothing could go wrong, not with him around.

Catherine looked over at the woman with the lab coat. Catherine had some many questions she needed to ask, but as she saw Tennessee getting to her feet, she could only think of one.

"Faith?" Catherine asked. Tennessee shook her head, keeping her eyes on the floor.

Catherine looked back at Sue, whose eyes went over to the Briggs Boys, "Tell us everything," Sue said.

11

I THINK YOU SHOULD JUST CALM DOWN

PLANET DEAD

"So, we set the place on fire, grabbed the doctor, and headed here." Robert's voice was fading in and out of Catherine's ears as she continued loading bullets into her magazine.

Catherine's eyes washed over her husband, who smiled the whole way through his story. She wanted to get lost in his tale, to get lost in his husky sweet voice, but every other moment she could see that her eyes weren't the only ones entranced by her husband's tale.

In a dirty white coat, standing in a corner away from the group, was the doctor. Her eyes kept glaring over at Robert. There was a feeling in the air and, as Catherine slammed the final bullet into her magazine, her eyes and the doctor's eyes met. In that moment, the feeling became clear. The doctor's eyes quickly broke away from Catherine's.

There was something going on. Catherine could smell it.

"So, you and Doctor Giggles were just gonna fly off into the sunset together?" Catherine asked. Letting her back rest on the wall, she laughed. "Here I am, walking miles, fighting zombies, getting fucking kidnapped!"

"Y'all got kidnapped?" Peter asked.

Catherine looked over and nodded as she childishly mocked, "Yes, we got kidnapped!" She stood up and started making a beeline to Robert.

"I did everything to find you! I did everything and you didn't even look for me? You didn't even stop to wonder if I was alive?"

Catherine's words were meant to be cold and vicious, but each new question left her lips sounded more hurt than the last.

"He looked for you," Doctor Brooks said softly.

Tennessee laughed and shook her head. "Yeah, I don't think you get to talk. You get to cry, maybe run, you damn sure get the opportunity to be knocked the fuck out, but I don't think you get to talk sweetheart."

Sue walked up, putting herself between Catherine and Robert; she stared at Catherine and said, "Look at me." Tearfully, Catherine turned her head as Sue softly said, "I don't know who she is, but what I do know..." Sue's hand went up to Catherine's cheek, "Is he looked for you."

Catherine's eyes started to water; she shook her head and went to rush off, but she was stopped by Jordan's arms wrapping around her. "We never stopped looking," he said and, as his words hit her ears, Robert's arms consumed her from behind.

"That's beautiful! I love it, you're happy, he's happy. The world's a beautiful fucking place! Now can we get back to the part where Doctor Hoe Pants has a way out?" Tennessee's words ripped through to soft moment.

"You're a bitch, you know that?" Sue said

"I am not sleeping with Robert!" The Doctor shouted out like a child having a tantrum. Her hands were balled up into fists. She slowly started to release her trapped fingers as the moment faded. Doctor Brooks did not enjoy the feeling of being ignored. Her biggest issue in life was feeling like people didn't listen to her, but now everyone was staring at her. She looked over at Peter and stomped her foot. "Peter!" she cried.

Robert's brother slowly put his hand up in the air with a light smile. "She's my...umm girl?" he said, puzzled for a moment, before adding, "Well, we ain't talked labels yet."

Sue folded her arms over her chest, and Tennessee laughed. "Why didn't you say something?" Sue asked softly.

Peter looked over at Catherine as he shrugged and said, "Kitty Cat scares me."

"*D*on't call me that," Catherine said. She broke free of her boys and walked over to the Doctor; their eyes met again and, just like before, the doctor's eyes quickly broke away. When she was in a courtroom and the witness's eyes would cut away, that was as good as a signed confession in Catherine's mind. Some people could stare you in the eyes and tell you the sky is green, but other people just weren't made for secrets.

"What's the plan?" Catherine asked.

Doctor Brooks folded her arms over her chest as she said, "That's it?" She laughed and pointed over her shoulder at Tennessee. "You and your guard dog here owe me an apology"

Tennessee put her hand up and closed her eyes as she said, "Excuse me, Doctor Hoe Pants, I don't believe the name calling is necessary. We've moved on."

Catherine rolled her eyes and bit down on her lip. She let out a sigh, but right before the words left her lips, the lights went out.

"Oh no, no, no," Doctor Brooks softly said as she pushed past Catherine and started running down the hallway. Everyone one raced after her, but when Tennessee started down the hallway, she felt a hand slam into her chest stopping her cold.

Catherine stepped forward till her and Tennessee were face to face; she felt Tennessee's heart pounding under her touch for a moment before she dropped her hand.

"This is the second time you've left with someone and came back alone," Catherine said.

"Are you fucking kidding me?" Tennessee said.

She gave Catherine a light push and whispered, "What the hell do you think I did?"

Catherine's head went to the side and she smiled. "Don't touch me."

"Don't touch you? You're ass wasn't saying that when I patched you up!" Tennessee shouted as she pointed at Catherine's bandage. "You think I killed her?" she said.

"What I think is that Faith and Adam aren't here," Catherine said.

"Faith bled out and Adam got eaten!" Tennessee said.

"Blood," Catherine said softly.

"What?" Tennessee asked.

"You said Adam got attacked by a zombie in the truck, but if he did..." Catherine stepped forward and stared into Tennessee's eyes. Red lights were flashing around them. The sun shined down through the skylight. They stood there, dirty, bloody and broke much like the rest of the world, "Where was the blood?" Catherine finally asked.

Tennessee stared. It was a blank stare. She didn't seemed worried or phased by the question; in fact, she seemed like she knew it was coming.

"I didn't do it," Tennessee said softly.

Catherine looked down the hall. "We're gonna regroup and get the hell out of this fucking state," she softly said, glaring back at Tennessee, "and then we'll talk about why people seem to end up dead around you."

Catherine started walking backwards slowly then she turned around and ran down the hall leaving Tennessee alone under the skylight.

"Oh, we'll talk. We'll talk real soon," Tennessee whispered to herself.

THESE ARE THE FACTS AS WE KNOW THEM

PLANET DEAD

"Maxine!" Peter hollered.

Footsteps echoed down the hallway as Peter and the others raced behind Doctor Maxine Brooks, who was turning corner after corner as she mumbled repeatedly to herself, "No, No, No."

Each time the word left her lips she swore a bit of her sanity went with it.

"Maxine!" Peter shouted every few moments in hopes of pulling her out of her crazed race of panic. His feet turned one last corner to find Maxine standing in front of a glass door.

The doctor stood there with her head pressed against the cool glass of the sliding door. Her fist slammed into the glass as she screamed, "Fuck!" Her hand came back quickly, shaking back and forth through the air as her eyes started to water.

Peter stopped a few feet behind her as the others started to catch up. Sue's arms were wrapped around her midsection as she slowly started to slide down a nearby wall to the floor. Sue's eyelids wrinkled as she squeezed them shut.

"You alright?" the voice pulled Sue away from the pain only

for a moment as she looked up to see Catherine. Sue nodded and put her hand out letting Catherine pull her to her feet.

"You took a beating back there, Sue. Maybe you should hang back."

Sue smiled. "I'm fine, I just wanna get the hell out of here."

"We all do," Robert said.

Catherine looked over at the Doctor, who was running her fingers down the glass door. "Your girl over there doesn't seem to care about leaving," Catherine said.

Peter started walking toward Doctor Brooks. "Y'all chill," he said. He stood behind her and looked at the glass before softly saying, "This where you left him?" Brooks turned her head to look at Peter giving him a slight nod before looking back at the glass.

"But something setoff the security protocol. The whole building is in lockdown," Brooks said. She took her glasses off and screamed tossing her head back. "Fuck!" Peter put his hand on her shoulder and she quickly slapped it away. "You don't get it! This was our only way out. If we don't have him, then there's no hope of anyone coming to get us."

Peter shook his head. "We got Jordan, you said the little man is like the second coming of Zombie cures, right?"

Doctor Brooks looked over at the little boy and nodded, but then shook her head, "Yes, Jordan's blood has all the markers to my work but Patient Zero—"

"Jordan has all the what?" Catherine's voice pushed through the bickering.

Tennessee slowly stepped from around the corner to reunite with the group, folding her arms over her chest staring at the survivors. A small smile creeped up onto her face, then her eyes lowered to see Jordan staring at her. Tennessee blew the little boy a kiss before he turned back around.

"What the hell does my son have to do with all this?" Catherine asked.

Doctor Brooks ran her fingers through her hair, tossing the brown waves into a shaggy mess as she let out a loud sigh.

"This infection is highly contagious, and extremely volatile." She pushed her hands into her dirty lab coat as she started to walk into the center of the group. "People like you and me, if an infected individual's blood or any bodily fluid for that matter, gets into our system, then we have one of two paths. We slowly die as our core temperature heats up and we cook from the inside out or we internally cook just long enough to fry most of our brain cells and become—"

"A zombie," Sue said.

Brooks shook her head. "I wouldn't really call them zombies. There's no such thing,"

Tennessee laughed and pointed over her shoulder. "You gonna go outside and tell them that?"

Doctor Brooks looked at Peter. "We went over this. These are not reanimated corpses. They're infected human beings with a high amount of—"

Catherine placed two fingers to her lips and let out a loud whistle, she looked around at all the eyes on her. "Get the fuck back on track. Who cares what y'all wanna call them?"

Doctor Brooks nodded and pushed her glasses up with her finger as she said, "While we fall victim to the infection, there seem to be people who are immune to it all together. At first, we thought Patient Zero might have been the only case, but, after my forced cooperation with the military, we came across your family and Jordan, who seems to have the same markers of being immune to the infection."

Robert rubbed his hand on Jordan's head. "She thinks she can make a vaccine out of the little man's blood and save the world." Robert's words made Tennessee laugh.

Tennessee rolled her eyes before being elbowed by Sue. "What? I don't give two shits about saving the world. That's not what I'm here for."

Catherine's eyes fell onto Tennessee. She wanted to scream, 'What the fuck are you here for then?' The thought of dragging Tennessee down the hall by her hair and beating some answers out of her crossed Catherine's mind. But, as her eyes came back to Jordan's shaggy mess of hair, she remembered why she was here.

"And this Patient Zero is locked up in there?" she asked.

Doctor Brooks nodded and started walking back toward the glass door. "The system went into lockdown. Something must have set it off." Brooks looked over her shoulder at Catherine, "We came here to get Zero and rendezvous with the chopper on the roof in..." She looked down at the watch on her hand her closed her eyes, "Forty minutes."

Catherine looked over at Sue and Tennessee, and then her eyes made it over to the Briggs boys before saying, "And this chopper can hold how many?" Brooks looked back at the glass and Catherine snapped her fingers. "I asked you a question Doctor!"

There was an awkward silence that took over the hall. The doctor's eyes dropped to the floor and finally Catherine knew just what the bloody elephant in the room was. Catherine looked at Robert and stared into his brown eyes as his hand ran down his beard, tugging at it as he let out a sigh.

"The Manifest is for five including Zero. It's not gonna hold all of us," Robert answered.

Peter's head turned toward his brother as he shouted, "Us? What you talking about us? We talking about 'us' as in us or 'us' as in them?"

Sue raised an eyebrow and said, "Real nice Pete! You just gonna leave us here to die?"

Peter looked over at Robert and then over at Doctor Brooks before he started to laugh. "Nah, I was just making sure we weren't leaving y'all behind. One team, one fight," Peter said with a smile.

Catherine rolled her eyes before taking a step forward. She grabbed the Doctor and spun her around before softly saying, "You seem like a nice girl, and I'm sorry about that whole mess back there earlier." Brooks scoffed and Catherine closed her eyes. "But we all came a long way and if all of us aren't leaving," Catherine's eyes popped open and she whispered, "None of us are."

Brooks could feel Catherine's fingers digging into her arms through the lab coat. Catherine's hazel eyes were locked on the doctor for a moment, before releasing her slowly.

"Now," Catherine clapped her hands together and looked at her little ragtag group, "The Doctor here is gonna figure out how to get us all the hell out of here—"

Brooks shook her head, "You people aren't listening. This escape is only happening if we have Patient Zero."

Catherine rolled her head slowly over toward the Doctor's direction as she mockingly said "Oh really? Is it not happening without him?"

Sue laughed for a moment, before her hand shot to her side trying to fight the pain.

"We'll get your little lab rat out of his cage. Just make sure you get us all a ride out of here," Catherine said

Catherine walked up to Jordan and gave the boy a kiss on the cheek. "No," Jordan said.

Catherine smiled. "I haven't even said anything yet."

Jordan shook his head, closing his eyes. "No, I'm coming with you."

Catherine smiled and shook her head. "No you're not. You're gonna stay here and watch after Sue, she's in bad shape."

Catherine stared at Jordan and then put her arm around the little boy, she pressed his head into her midsection and took a deep sigh as she said, "You know how much I missed you?" Jordan nodded slowly and then Catherine stepped back to look at her son. "I did some crazy stuff to get to you."

Jordan softly said, "I know, Ma."

"And I'm not gonna lose you again." She kissed the shaggy headed boy right in the middle of his black mess of hair.

Sue waved her hands and started walking over before coming to a stop and leaning on a nearby wall. Catherine walked over to her and she ran her finger through the girl's hair. "We're all going," Sue said.

Catherine shook her head before leaning in and whispering, "I don't trust her."

Sue looked over at Doctor Brooks and then whispered, "The Doctor?"

Catherine leaned back and shouted, "Tennessee! You and I are gonna go figure out how to get this door open."

Tennessee looked around for a moment and then looked back at Catherine as her finger came up and pointed at herself. "We're gonna what?"

Catherine walked over to her. "We're gonna get the door open."

Tennessee laughed. "I'm not sure I'm the best choice."

Catherine stood in front of Tennessee. She stared at the young woman's dark black hair and soft pale skin before she smiled and said, "Sweetie, you're the only choice."

"I'm going with you."

Catherine's eyes slowly pulled away from Tennessee to land on her husband and his shaggy beard. He stood to the side of the two women with his M4 held tightly in his hand. She went to shake her head, but he placed his hand on the side of her neck and rubbed his fingers along the soft part where her neck and jawline met. He pulled her in for a deep kiss.

Catherine had forgotten how amazing it felt, how earth shattering it was just to feel the lips of another against her own. She held her eyes closed, as if this was a dream she never wanted to end. Yet, when Robert's lips broke away from hers, he said, "I'm coming with you and that's the end of that."

Catherine nodded slowly in her lovesick daze. Peter unslung his weapon and held it out to Tennessee. "Here take this," he said.

Catherine watched as the weapon left Peter's fingers and rested in Tennessee light pale hands. Tennessee smiled and Catherine looked over at Peter. "You guys might need it," she said.

Peter lifted his shirt to show two handguns pushed between his belt and his abs, "Nah, we good. Y'all be safe, because if what Maxine is saying is right, then—"

Robert nodded and looked over at Catherine who pulled back the charging handle on her weapon letting a bullet jump into the chamber.

"Then what?" Sue asked.

Catherine's head turned toward the young woman as she said, "We're not alone."

13

IT OPENED ITS EYES

PLANET DEAD

"Sooo." Robert's voice broke through the dark silence as their footsteps echoed throughout the halls of the CDC. The sun was starting to set now, but Catherine had no way of knowing that because she was in the heart of the building now.

There were no windows, just dark corner after dark corner as the red emergency lights on the walls flashed constantly. Catherine held her flashlight tightly along the barrel of the M4 and led the way into the darkness.

"So, what?" Catherine asked.

"So, how did you and Sue end up together?" Robert asked softly.

Tennessee laughed, causing the light to swing around blinding her. "What the fuck are you laughing at?" Catherine shouted.

Tennessee put her hand up, trying to block out the light. "Take it easy, Killer. I was just making a gay joke in my head."

Robert laughed looking over at Catherine as he said, "That's funny."

Catherine turned the light around and continued walking as she softly said, "No, it's not."

A few moments of silence past till out of the darkness came the entire gory tale. "We found each other. Then we found Tennessee and—"

~

"And then she found out Sue knew where you guys were the whole time," Tennessee said.

Faith's blood was still fresh on her hands and Tennessee knew Faith was still running through Catherine's mind. So, the best thing for the both of them was to keep Faith dead and buried until they could have their talk.

Catherine came to a stop and looked around the hallway. "We need to get to the basement."

Tennessee rolled her shoulders as she let the heavy rifle hang around her body. "Why?"

Catherine pointed the light down another hallway. "Because from the basement we can cut the power to the building."

Robert nodded. "Yeah, then we can kick the power back on and hopefully negate the security system."

"And that's gonna work?" Tennessee asked.

Catherine shrugged her shoulders as she started down the hallway. "Maybe. It works with the copy machine at work."

"Okay, I mean just as long as you two know what you're doing." Tennessee looked around for a moment before saying, "On an unrelated note, if I wanted out of this shit show, which way would be the exit?"

"Shut the hell up," Catherine said.

"I looked for you," Robert said softly.

Catherine looked over her shoulder as she said, "You shut the hell up too," and continued to walk down the dark hallway.

"I did. We traced your cellphone. We found your car in the river."

Catherine came to a stop when she heard those words. The light was shining down the white hallway as Robert continued, "I jumped in. I don't know what I thought I was gonna find." Robert stopped and ran his hand over his face. "I kept telling myself I was just seconds behind you. I was sure I'd pull you from the water. I was sure I'd save you."

"Stop." Catherine's soft voice echoed down the hallway and the pain in her words shook through the walls.

Robert's hand went up to Catherine's shoulder, then his hand slowly ran along her skin, making their way to a spot on the back of her neck. His finger traced it and a chill ran down Catherine's back.

"I went deeper and deeper. I saw those things, all fighting to get at me. Every few seconds, I would hope to see your eyes, but all I saw was the dead," he said.

Robert took a step forward and, as his bread brushed against Catherine's ear, she smiled. His lips parted and he whispered, "I would have looked through those waters forever, I would have looked for you forever, but Jordan..."

When she heard Jordan's name Catherine's smile faded. She wanted to tell Robert it was okay. That she understood. That she would have done the same thing. Catherine wanted to say so many things, but instead she heard a deafening shriek break through the darkness of the halls.

Catherine's rifle came up and the beam of light scanned the dead halls that surrounded them. The sound grew louder and Catherine's rifle fell from her fingers and hit the floor. She covered her ears, dropping the flashlight to the ground. As the flashlight spun along the floor, Catherine, Robert, and Tennessee, covering their ears as well. Tennessee was on her knees, screaming through the pain, and Robert was just moments away from doing the same.

Catherine pressed on her ears as tight as she could, her eyes shut as a throbbing sensation filled her skull. She dropped to her knees screaming alongside Tennessee. Their cries of torment were nothing compared to the howls that were echoing through the halls of the CDC, but just as suddenly as it started, it stopped.

Robert's hands slowly came down from his ears to reveal little droplets of blood in his palms. His hands quickly went back to his ears, his fingers snapping loudly by his skull. Robert's head slowly came up with a smile.

"I think I'm okay!" Robert's words echoed along the hall as Catherine started to get back to her feet.

"What the fuck is that!" Tennessee's finger shot out as a figure sped past the beam of the flashlight.

Catherine's body spun around quickly; she stared down the hallway "I don't see—"

From the darkness emerged a small figure that took slow footsteps down the long hallway. Catherine shot forward grabbing her rifle and the flashlight. She watched as the small thing in a medical robe slowly made its way toward them.

"It's a little girl?" Tennessee said, puzzled.

"Honey, you alright?" Catherine called out to the child. Catherine started to take a step forward but felt a large hand pull her back by her arm. She looked back and saw Robert shaking his head.

The flashlight pointed at the girl and Catherine's eyes got a good look at what was standing before them. The girl's skin was pale and, as the light shined on her, Catherine swore she could see every vein running through her tiny body. It was like she was translucent with a grayish red tint of color to her. There was also no hair on the child's body, nothing on her arms, her legs, nor her head. Her skin was drawn in tightly around her frame, showing every pointy bone that poked through the bloodstained robe. Dark red veins ran along her face and a trail of hidden blood followed behind her, partly hidden by her shadow.

"She's infected," Robert whispered as he started raising his rifle.

Catherine took a step back as she tossed the flashlight behind her to Tennessee. "Here take this." Catherine raised the barrel of her rifle alongside Robert's.

"And what if she's not?" Tennessee asked.

Catherine's cheek found its way to the black metal and she pinned the butt-stock in her shoulder joint as she said, "You see all that fucking blood?" Her eye focused as it rested by the scoop and she could see the red triangle rest above the little girl's head like a party hat. "The kid's dead."

Tennessee smiled and nodded. "Shoot first and ask questions later, right? I mean, it's not like we're all covered in blood or anything."

Catherine looked over at Robert and then back at Tennessee. She bit her lip and shouted, "Honey!" Catherine's eyes went back toward the girl as she raised her rifle up to her cheek and took aim. "You alright!"

The shuffling of her bare feet along the white tile came to an eerie stop. Tennessee stood there with the flashlight pinned on the girl who was breathing heavily. The only sound that could be heard was the inhale and exhale from her tiny body until the metal click of Robert's bullet being chambered into his barrel filled the air.

The girl's head jerked back, allowing the group to see a pair of dark black eyes surrounded by a river of reddish gray skin. The girl's mouth grew wide, revealing bloodstained jagged teeth as another high pitch wail reverberated around them. The sound was haunting and painful. It felt as if there were hundreds of them doing it due to it echoing through the halls.

The light quickly came off the girl as Tennessee covered her ears.

Catherine took aim at the girl once again, tightened her finger, and pulled back on the trigger. The blast did its best to battle against the scream. The bullet flew through the air and connected with the middle of the girl's skull, sending her body flying down the hall. As the body fell limp among the blood trail in the hall, Catherine's rifle lowered.

"That's new," Robert said.

Another shriek was heard from down the hall, followed by another and another.

"We need to go!" Tennessee shouted.

"We need to get to the basement!" Catherine said as a cluster of sprinting footsteps echoed through the halls. Catherine raised her rifle again and Tennessee watched as Robert and Catherine started making their way deeper into the darkness of the hallway.

Tennessee shook her head. "Fuck!"

Moving slowly behind Mr. and Mrs. Briggs. The darkness in the center of the hall was cast out by the flashlight as they turned the corner. Then they saw it, in bright green letters just hanging in the air.

"It's the exit!" Tennessee rushed forward but quickly came to a halt as Robert's hand blocked her escape.

The stairwell was only a few feet away. Yet, they were frozen in place by the sight of gray faces and black eyes racing toward them. Blood coated the approaching mouths and the shrieks grew louder.

Catherine's hands were composed and ready, but her heart was slamming around in her chest. Some had robes like the little girl, others had lab coats, military uniforms, and normal everyday attire, as if they'd just stepped in off the street. They all shared the same pulsating blood vessels and bald heads that cut in and out of the light as the screeching got louder.

The trio brought their weapons up and Catherine opened

up fire, sending one lead bullet after another into the infected crowd that swarmed them.

"What the fuck is this?" Catherine screamed out.

"There's so many of them!" Tennessee hollered over the bullets.

"Stop talking and keep shooting!" Robert said. "We'll push them back and make a run for the door!"

With every bullet they fired, they moved closer and closer toward the exit sign. As the first wave of infected were shot down, the second wave seemed to have watched and learned. Many of them began to race toward them zigzagging back and forth through the light. Headshots became damn near impossible, so they took whatever shot they could get. Bullet after bullet was being fired. The bodies went down and then sprung back up as if nothing happened.

"Get to the door!" Robert shouted as he moved closer to the pack of infected. "I'll hold them back!"

Tennessee wasted no time. She put one foot in front of the other and took off racing toward the door. With her went the light, leaving Catherine and Robert behind to face the monsters in the darkness. As her hands pushed the door open, Tennessee felt her body being ripped back from the doorway. Her hands slammed onto the doorframe and she screamed, "Get off me!"

Catherine's barrel turned toward the doorway and she pulled back on the trigger, sending a bullet cutting through the air. Unlike the barrage of random shots she and Robert had been dishing out, this one found its mark, blasting a hole in the side of the zombie's skull.

Tennessee took her newfound freedom and bolted through the doorway and down the steps.

"Let's go!" Catherine said, but Robert continued firing into the pack unphased by his wife's request. "Let's go, Robert!" Catherine shouted again.

"I'll lay down cover fire as—" His words got cut off by the sound of Catherine's rifle firing shot after shot as she switched her M4 to three-round bursts. The barrel smoked as it sprayed from left to right, pushing the wave of infected back. Catherine watched as the bodies dropped to the floor only to get back on their feet within a matter of seconds.

They were fighting a losing battling, Robert could see that now. "Fine, on three!"

"One," Catherine said as the bullets whizzed through the hall.

"Two," Robert shouted over the gunfire.

The two of them turned and bolted for the door as they both screamed out, "Three!"

Catherine's shoulder bashed into the metal of the door, sending it flying open. She kept her eyes forward and her feet moving, skipping one step after another. Her hands locked onto the railings in hopes of keeping her body from stumbling down the staircase. Catherine's only focus was getting away, until she heard it.

"Fuck!" Robert's smooth, deep voice shouted out the word. His back was pressed up against the door as the infected began to pummel the metal. The leather of his boots did their best to hold their ground, but, with each hit, Robert felt himself sliding back.

Catherine darted back up the steps. "Robert!"

Robert put out his hand. "Just keep going, someone has to hold them back!"

Catherine stood at the bottom of the staircase and stared up at her husband. His arms and back were pinned against the door. His eyes were closed tightly trying to avoid her light brown gaze, one that he thought he would never see again.

Catherine shook her head and Robert shouted, "Just go!"

"I'm not leaving you!" Catherine said, she put her foot on

the step and her fingers wrapped around the handle of her weapon.

When Robert's eyes opened they were staring down the barrel of Catherine's rifle, "So you're gonna kill me! Kitty Cat, we can talk about this," Just then another zombie slammed into the metal door and his hold weakened.

"Don't call me that!" Catherine said as she took a deep breath and then blew it out of the corner of her mouth. She pressed her cheek to black metal and her eye to the scope. "Run and don't look back," she said.

Robert shook his head. "No! Catherine, just keep—"

Robert's words were cut off by Catherine sending a bullet into the upper part of the door; his head ducked, and his eyes quickly went toward his wife.

"Are you crazy?" he shouted.

Catherine bellowed back. "Move!"

Robert's dog tags were rising and falling quickly as they rested on his chest. He held his weapon close and then let out a big sigh followed by, "You're so fucking hardheaded," as he released the door and started running.

Catherine opened up fire into the crowd of infected, that were trying to force their way through the door. One head shot after another and another. Catherine had dropped three zombies before the crowd finally pushed their way through. Wide eyed and heart racing, Catherine leapt down the staircase and started running.

Robert was turning back every few seconds to fire off shots. They came to a dark stairway, their footsteps lost in the thundering sound of the infected chasing them through what seemed like a never-ending staircase. They ran deeper into the darkness when a door flew open, shining a bright white light on them.

"What the hell took you two so long?" Tennessee said.

Robert and Catherine rushed through the open door.

Tennessee slammed the door shut and turned the deadbolt, locking it. A loud pounding could be heard from the other side of the metal. Tennessee frantically started backing up with the flashlight. "What the fuck are those things?" she asked.

Catherine's hands went on the top of her head as she did her best to ease the fire that had taken over her lungs.

"Zombies?" Robert asked.

Tennessee shined the light in the Robert's face. "Bullshit. Zombies aren't that fucking fast and they don't all sport the same hair do." She ran her fingers through her hair before point back at the door. "Did you see any bites? Any fucking cuts on them? Because I didn't!"

Catherine closed her eyes and said, "Look for a fuse box or a generator."

Tennessee's head spun toward Catherine. "No! What the fuck are they?" She demanded.

"I don't know! And right now, I don't fucking care!" Catherine shouted back.

She turned to look around the dimly lit room. "All I know is they're waiting for us to get that lab open and that's what we're gonna do. That's the mission."

Tennessee pointed the flashlight in Catherine's face; blinding her for a moment. Catherine closed her eyes as orange spots slowly moved around in the darkness. She listened to Tennessee's footsteps slowly moving away.

"You alright?" Catherine's eyes opened to see the red glow of the room shining down on Robert's face. She went to slap him, but the impact was blocked by his forearm. "What the hell?" Robert said.

Catherine slapped him with her free hand, "What the hell is wrong with you, Robert!" She broke loose, then she started slapping and punching wildly. The blows got weaker and softer, then she wasn't hitting him at all. She was resting her head on his chest and crying. "What the hell is wrong with you?"

Robert's cheek settled on the top of Catherine's soft jet-black hair. His eyes closed and his lips parted. "I'm sorry."

The two of them stood there, wrapped in one another's arms, until the pounding on the door became too hard to ignore. Catherine's head came up and she wiped away her tears before turning and saying, "Let's go."

Walking down a dark hallway, Tennessee shined her light along the walls revealing several unmarked doors, with large padlocks on them. A hand grabbed hold of Tennessee's shoulder causing her to jump and drop the flashlight. "What the fuck!"

Catherine leaned down picking up the light. "Sorry, what'd you find?".

The light came back up on the padlock and Tennessee shook her head. "I don't like this."

Robert nodded as he raised his weapon, "Neither do I."

Catherine's hand reached for the lock and, as her fingers got closer, the metal the door started to violently shake. The three of them watched as the lock pushed and pulled against the metal latch. Catherine took a step back.

"We need to get the fuck out of here," she said and looked over at Tennessee and Robert. "Like now!"

They quickly continued down the hallway. "What the hell were they doing in this place?" Tennessee asked Catherine.

Rising her weapon, Catherine felt Tennessee following closely behind her. "Nothing good,"

Robert stopped cold. "Shit! You think Brooks knew about this?"

Tennessee laughed and shook her head. "Oh no, I doubt she knew anything about the super zombies or the creepy basement." She rolled her eyes, "I mean, it's not like she works here or anything."

Robert looked over at Catherine. "Who the hell is she again?" he asked.

Catherine stopped as the flashlight shined on an open doorway. Robert and Tennessee came up beside her. The trio stared into the bright beam of light that showed two concrete steps leading down into a room.

"You think one of them got out?" Tennessee asked.

Catherine shook her head as she handed the flashlight to Tennessee. She raised her weapon and walked through the doorway, down the steps.

"Give me some light," Catherine said.

Tennessee pointed the light over Catherine's shoulder, revealing a dusty room with pipes running along the ceiling. The light scanned the room showing four large burners and two large grey metal panels.

"Go back!" Catherine said. The light quickly shot back to the metal panels. "Jackpot!" Catherine said with a smile.

"It's about time something good happened to us," Robert said. He cautiously walked in behind his wife, his weapon at the ready.

"That's it?" Tennessee asked.

Catherine unslung her weapon and rested it on the wall as she popped open the lids to the two panels, revealing rows of black switches. Catherine nodded. "Fuck yeah, it is!"

Tennessee laughed and leaned in the doorway. "Thank God! I'm so ready to get out of this place."

Robert walked up to the second box and put his hand on the top breaker switch as Catherine placed her hand on the other switch. The couple looked at each other. This was what they had been waiting for, what they had been fighting for. The final moment before their nightmare came to an end. Yes, there were still many questions to answer. Still battles that needed to be fought, but what mattered was they could fight them together. Robert leaned in and kissed his wife as they both pulled their switches to off.

The red lights went out and Tennessee dropped the flashlight to the ground. It rolled down the two steps, then spun along the cement floor. Its light fell onto Catherine, then the boilers, then Tennessee. They both pushed the switches back into the on position, causing the main lights to kick back on. Robert leaned back opening his eyes as he smiled at his wife.

"I love you," he said.

"I love you more," Catherine replied.

She looked over at Tennessee with a smile and froze. Then, Catherine's eyes got wide, her jaw started to fall open as she readied herself to scream, but her words couldn't match the pace of that moment. Tennessee was aiming her M4 in their direction. A roaring blast echoed through the small boiler room. Catherine's eyes were locked on Tennessee's finger pulling back on the trigger for a second time.

Robert's body jolted back, slamming into the fuse box. His knees buckled and his hand reached out to Catherine. Blood started cascading down his back onto the floor; his body followed a second later. Robert's body fell over in a heap, surrounded by a mass of blood that took over the once gray concrete floor.

"Robert!" Catherine screamed.

She quickly rushed to her husband's side only to hear Tennessee shout, "No! You don't fucking move!"

Catherine stood still just inches away from Robert. She could see him from the corner of her eye. He wasn't screaming. His hands had fallen from his chest and into the puddle of blood. Catherine's eyes shot away from Tennessee down to Robert. She could see the two dark bullet holes in his body pushing out blood with every passing second. Catherine's eyes stung from the tears. Before she knew it, Robert's bloody body started to blur. She took a deep breath, then Catherine made a quick dash for her weapon.

Another blast echoed through the boiler room, which followed by a burning pain that rushed through Catherine's shoulder. She dropped down next to her rifle, her fingers just inches away. She pushed her hand forward brushing her fingertips along the butt-stock. Then Tennessee's heel came slamming down onto Catherine's fingers. Catherine screamed.

Tennessee laughed and twisted the heel of her boot, grinding Catherine's fingers into the concrete. The skin tore away, and Catherine felt the pain in her fingers battling the pain in her shoulder, both trying to take center stage in her mind.

"Well, now that we're alone, how about we have that talk," Tennessee said.

14

NOW WAIT A MINUTE

PLANET DEAD

*T*ap. Tap. Tap.

The sound of Maxine's nail tapping along the glass started off as a small annoyance and then quickly grew into the only thing Sue could think about, aside from wondering how Catherine was doing. Sue pulled her legs close to her. She rested her shoulder on the wall, unable to rest her back on much of anything. She bit down on her lip as the pain started to shoot through her again.

Sue's eyes closed trying to hold back the tears, but they slowly started to come. The darkness pulled her back to that farmhouse; she could smell the rotten scent that seemed to soak its way into the wood of the house. She could hear him laughing, just laughing. Sue's started breathing faster before she felt a hand touch her shoulder. She jumped and then wished she hadn't when the pain started running through her body again. Sue's eyes opened to see Peter and Jordan standing over her.

"You alright, blondie?" Peter asked, and Sue nodded her head.

"I'm fine." She slowly started to try to get to her feet, but the blood loss and the lack of food had her stumbling to the side; she almost fell over until she noticed the small arms that were holding her up. Her head turned to Jordan and she smiled. "You saved me again, kiddo," Sue said.

"Mom said to keep you safe," Jordan replied.

Peter nodded leaning on the wall, "Yeah, how the hell did you two end up together anyway?" Peter's arms folded over his chest. "Where's Samantha and Dean?"

Sue shook her head and looked down at the floor as she said, "They didn't make it."

Tap.

Tap.

Tap.

Sue's head leaned back as she shouted, "Do you have to fucking do that?"

Doctor Brooks' hand fell from the glass and she started to get to her feet as she said, "Sorry!"

Sue rolled her eyes and stood up straight. "How the hell are we gonna get out of here? Exactly?"

Brooks looked over at Peter and Peter looked at Sue. "There's a chopper that's coming, for zero so Maxine can make a cure." Peter said.

"There is no cure. The best we can do is make a vaccine for the virus," she said.

"So, they're coming for zero and four other doctors?" Sue asked.

Doctor Brooks ran her hands over her face. "This isn't how things were supposed to happen. I left to seek out more resources, I planned to return sooner but now..."

Sue turned her head to the side. "But now what?"

Brooks sighed as she said "It's possible they might have left or—"

"Or got eaten?" Sue asked. Sue looked over at Peter. "She's

full of it! There's no one coming. You heard her; they're gone or they're dead!"

Peter shook his head. "No, Max is gonna get us out. Tell her, Max."

Doctor Brooks' eyes went back toward the glass door and Sue rolled her eyes. "She's playing you. There are five spots on that chopper. Zero and her make," Sue's two fingers went up and wiggled. "In a building full of high-profile doctors, what the hell made you think she could get you a seat?" Sue asked.

Pete's eyes went from Sue to Doctor Brooks. "Max, tell her." The doctor didn't turn; she didn't give any hint that she'd even acknowledged Peter's words. "I said tell her, God damn it!"

"You would have been safe, but I'm needed elsewhere." The doctor's head turned to look at the trio. All eyes were on her as she shoved her hands in her pockets. "The chopper to the compound was set for tonight. Now, someone put the system into lockdown, so someone is here, which means it's still coming. Which means we can all go just as planned," she said.

"We can all go? So, you're gonna get us out of here?" Sue asked

"I'm not," Doctor Brook's replied.

Brooks's words filled up the red lit room, then the lights went out.

Sue shouted. "Excuse me bitch!?"

Peter's hands shot through the darkness and grabbed Sue, "Be easy blondie," Peter's words raced through Sue's mind and caused her to spin around on her heels. The rubber of her bloodstained white shoes squeaked as her hand balled up into a fist.

The lights shot back on and before Peter could react, Sue's fist came crashing into his nose.

"Don't call me that!" She screamed.

Peter stumbled backwards and shouted, "Son of a bitch!" as his hand covered his nose. His hand came down to reveal a palm full of blood, that quickly started spilling from his hands onto the white floor.

Sue took a step back as she started to rub her fist. "I'm sorry," she whispered to herself, while Peter held his head back attempting to stop the blood from flowing from his nose.

"Sorry? More like crazy, bitch," he shouted out and started walking over toward Dr. Brooks. "I think she broke my nose."

Sue and Jordan stood there as they watched Dr. Brooks gently start to care for Peter's injury. Sue rubbed her hands together and let out a sigh before saying, "What do you mean, you're not?"

Dr. Brooks ignored the question, she grabbed Peter's hand and walked him over to the glass door.

"Hello! I'm talking to you!" Sue shouted.

Dr. Brooks's hand quickly went up as she pressed her plastic keycard against the scanner pad. The glass door slide open and a computerized woman's voice filled the room as it said, "Welcome, Dr. Brooks. There is a message from Dr. Connors. Would you like me to play it?"

Dr. Brooks's stormed into the room pulling Peter alongside her as she said, "No, Speck"

"Who the hell is Speck?" Sue shouted.

She was about to step into the lab when she felt someone grab her hand and pull her back. Sue turned to see Jordan holding her hand staring up at her.

"Did you hear that?" Jordan asked.

Sue raised her eyebrow and looked down the bright white hallway. "Hear what?"

Jordan turned around and softly said, "I thought I heard a scream."

Sue brushed her hair from over her ears and listened for a moment, then shook her head. "I don't hear anything."

The boy's eyes didn't tear away from the bright white of the hallway. "It was a scream."

Sue put her hand on his cheek. "Your mom is fine, kiddo. If anyone is gonna come out of this okay, it's her."

Jordan smiled. "What about dad?"

Sue stuck her tongue out before saying, "Him too. We're all gonna be okay."

She started walking into the lab with Jordan right on her heels.

Peter sat on a table with his head back as Dr. Brooks softly applying a bandage to his nose.

"Fuck," Peter said softly.

Dr. Brooks smiled. "You're such a baby."

Sue stood there holding Jordan's hand. "Who's Speck?" Sue asked.

Dr. Brooks rolled her eyes with a sigh. "She's the artificial intelligence that helps run the lab."

Sue looked up at the lights of the ceiling, but before she could part her lips to respond, she heard Dr. Brooks's voice.

"When the White House fell, the government came to us for an explanation. They wanted answers or better put, they wanted someone to blame." Dr. Brooks pulled off her gloves and tossed them into a nearby trash bin, "Do you know how hard it is to come up with an answer for a question no one has ever asked?"

The doctor's eyes jumped from each of their faces and she laughed. "Of course you don't." she said as her hands went onto her hips. "We were tasked to find who or what created these monsters, all while figuring out how to stop them. Not save them, stop them. The government had already given up hope for a cure; they just wanted to know the best way to put an end to the country's nightmare."

"You're doing a lot of talking, but you're not really saying anything."

Sue's eyes went down to the little voice that pushed out the statement.

Jordan was staring at the Doctor as Peter laughed. "The kid's a savage."

Dr. Brooks pushed up her glasses and said, "We were given an unimaginable task. Passed down by the president himself, there were four doctors selected to head this up. Given what we've been through, I can explain bringing three people to the compound, but I can't explain anymore. My seat is barely safe!"

"What's the compound?" Sue asked.

Before the doctor could answer, a high-pitched scream echoed through the halls behind them.

Jordan's head spun around and he said, "There it goes again! Did you hear it?"

Sue's eyes were fixed on the glass door as she whispered, "We need to move."

The group stood there listening to the screams and Sue's head spun around as she shouted, "I said, we need to move, damn it!"

With that, Dr. Brooks feet took off through the lab and the rest followed. "We need to get Patient Zero to the roof!"

The doctor reached the doorway and pulled out her keycard; she pressed it against a black pad until she heard the click of the white wall pushing open.

"Help me," Sue heard a soft voice say.

When her eyes made it into the room, she saw a young Spanish man hanging off the side of a hospital bed. There was blood dripping from his arm onto the floor, blood that Dr. Brooks almost slipped in as she raced toward his bedside.

"What the fuck is going on!" Sue shouted.

The man turned his head to stare at the doctor. His light brown eyes locked with hers. The man's stubbled jaw started to tighten. He shot up, but, before his hands could make it to the doctor, she jammed a needle into his shoulder. The young man screamed and slapped the needle away, causing Dr. Brooks to jump back.

"Peter!" she shouted.

Peter sprung forward, pinning the young man to the bed. He bucked and writhed, violently swinging his hands to break free of Peter's hold. He was fighting for his life when suddenly the movement stopped, and his body just fell limp onto the bed. His black curly hair overtook the white of the pillow.

Sue's eyes never broke away from the man. She moved closer to the bed as Peter and Dr. Brooks started to strap the man down. Sue's hand reached toward the man's bloody arm. The long metal needle had broken off and was lodged in his shoulder. When Sue's fingers got closer to it, her hand was slapped away by Dr. Brooks.

For a moment, they stared at one another. Sue searched Dr. Brooks's eyes for any form of empathy, but when Dr. Brooks shouted, "We need to get him up to the roof!" Sue knew there was none.

Another ear-splitting cry ran through the lab and Sue's head spun back to the glass door. Peter pulled the guns out from under his shirt and handed one to Sue.

"You get any better at shooting?"

Sue took the gun into her hand. "No, but I've gotten pretty good at not dying."

Peter nodded. "Well, that's better than nothing."

The two of them carefully moved toward the glass door. A heart-stopping screech filled up the room and Sue jumped back. Peter's hand covered Sue's gun. She didn't notice she was shaking until she felt Peter's touch.

"It's gonna be—" Pete got cut off by a small laugh from Sue.

"Don't say, 'It's gonna be okay;' nothing good comes after that."

Frantic footsteps slammed against the white tile floor as the hoard raced down the hall.

"Zombies?" Jordan asked softly.

The silver tip of Peter's handgun pointed at the doorway. "Stay behind us little man."

Sue pointed her gun and closed her eyes for a moment before letting out a slow sigh. When the last bit of air left her lips, she saw it. A bald gray-skinned man with thick broken glasses hanging around his face.

His eyes were bloodshot.

His head twisted to the side like a confused rabid Pitbull.

He stepped through the doorway.

He took off sprinting toward them.

The man's eyes were fixed on Sue, his twisted figure burning itself into her memory. She saw his bloody white lab coat dancing in the air as he ran toward them. Hanging barely by a clip from his coat was a plastic name tag. Dark black letters were lined up neatly on the white tag spelling out Dr. H. Connors. When Sue's eyes came up, she saw its bloodstained mouth rip open and produce a deafening scream.

Dr. Brooks' hands desperately covered her ears; she and Jordan both dropped their heads in hopes of avoiding the horrifying sound. But for Sue and Peter, there was no avoiding what was to come. That scream was the dinner bell and they were all on Dr. Connors' menu.

The first shot sounded...

Then the next...

Peter and Sue were releasing bullet after bullet as more of the infected started rushing through the doorway.

"Speck! Seal the lab!" Dr. Brooks screamed out over the gunfire.

With those words, the lab door started to slide close. Yet, the glass door came to a stop. It was blocked off by the bodies of the infected that were fighting their way in.

Sue started walking closer to the growing hoard, firing shot after shot into the infected swarm. She prayed for headshots but took whatever fate was kind enough to give her.

Losing Samantha and Dean...

Being chased through the woods...

Meeting those fucking clowns.

All the hell Sue had been through was racing through her mind as she pulled her finger back on the trigger and let another bullet fly through the air.

"I am so sick of fucking Zombies!" Sue screamed.

The sliding door finally slid close and when it did, a wave of blood splashed onto Sue's shirt. The glass door was dark red as it crushed the rib cage of the infected, slicing it in half.

Sue watched the blood gushing from the thing's torso. It had one arm and still it continued to drag itself toward Sue. She heard another shot. The bullet went right through the man's skull and the infected torso dropped onto the blood-covered floor. Sue's head turned back to see Peter staring at her.

"Did you get your little Rambo moment out of your system?" Peter asked.

Sue raised her eyebrow. "Okay, I keep hearing that. Who the hell is Rambo?"

Peter laughed and looked over at Dr. Brooks. "Which way out of here?"

Dr. Brooks came up from the ground slowly and looked around the lab. The black frames of her glasses fought against the shaking of her hands as she placed them on her face. She took a slow breath before she said, "We need to get to the elevator on the east wing of the complex, if we—"

A chilling metal click stopped the doctor cold; she carefully turned around to see the barrel of Sue's gun pointed at her face. The doctor slowly put her hand up.

Peter took a step forward and Sue softly said, "Don't move Pete." Sue's head motioned toward the bodies that lined the floor. "You get one shot to tell me what the fuck is going on here."

"We don't have time for this," Dr. Brooks said.

Sue pushed the gun forward until the barrel was pressing into the Doctor's forehead. "One shot! Before I take mine!" Sue shouted.

Dr. Brooks' eyes went toward Peter, who was being pulled back with every bit of force in Jordan's tiny body. Dr. Brooks looked back at Sue. "Get that thing out of my face."

"Sue, what the fuck!" Peter shouted.

Sue's right hand came off the gun and she pointed out into the mass of bodies that lined the floor, her eyes never swaying from the doctor. Catherine had some trust issues and Sue knew they were well-earned; Catherine's gut never seemed to be wrong. This time was no different, Catherine said she didn't trust her and now neither did Sue.

Peter's eyes scanned over the carcasses that littered that lab. Men, women, even a few children were piled there with twisted faces and bloody bared teeth. Peter took in the sight of leather tight, reddish gray skin. Their veins showed as bright and defined as a road map would, running all along their bodies.

Yet, it wasn't any of that which made Peter turn away. No, it was the black eyes, so dark and empty. He would never admit it, but those eyes were burned into his nightmares.

Peter looked back at Jordan only to hear Sue shout, "No! Keeping looking. Find the guy in the lab coat!" She started to back away from Dr. Brooks, making her way toward Jordan as she added, "His name tag says Connors."

Dr. Brooks's head turned toward the pile of bodies. Her eyes were racing from twisted to face to twisted face. Right in the middle of the lab, covered in blood, was Dr. Connors. Only recognizable by his thick black glasses and bullet-riddled white lab coat.

"No," Dr. Brooks softly said.

She went to move toward him, but Sue's barrel tapped the side of Brooks' head. The doctor looked back at Sue with tearful eyes.

"He doesn't deserve to lay there like some animal!" Dr. Brooks shouted.

"I want answers or you'll be laying right next to him," Sue said.

Dr. Brooks was glaring at Sue through the teary eyes, burning a hole into her. They were passed mistrust. Hate was slowly filling up the void between them.

Dr. Brooks's lips parted. "Play the message, Speck."

"Playing video message from Dr. Connors."

The lights in the lab dimmed and a blue hologram shot up in the middle. Blue and white light scrambled in the middle of the air as the screams and the pounding of the infected got louder. The bright glow of light engulfed Sue's face.

A bearded dark-skinned man with thick glasses appeared. He sat there, hands clasped over scattered paperwork. His eyes looked away for a moment then they shot back toward the group. His name tag was in plain view, just as clear now as it was moments before.

"Maxine, if you're listening to this, then it's too late." Dr. Connors ran his hands over his face and sighed into them for a moment. "I made a grave mistake Maxine."

The massive projection filled Sue's eye with the sight of short cut, wavy black hair, thick black framed glasses that amplified his two hazel eyes. Dr. Connors's fingers slid down his face, allowing his fingertips to drag along his shaggy black beard.

Dr. Connors started laughing softly. "So, you were right, like always. They pushed for us to mass produce the vaccine." He looked off camera for a second time, then he continued. "I don't have much time. Against my better judgement, I gave the vaccine to all personnel who were selected to depart for the compound. Including myself."

"Matthew, no." Dr. Brooks' words came out faintly as if they were never meant to be spoken at all. It was a tone of pain that she didn't want to share with another living soul.

Her words pulled Peter's eyes away from the projection and onto her. Dr. Brooks' hands pressed against her eyes as she felt the warm tears starting to flow.

"That was two weeks ago and the testing seemed positive. No negative impacts whatsoever. Two weeks!" Connors shouted, his fist slammed into the table. "We proceeded to administer the vaccine to the rest of the CDC personnel and civilians who made it in before the quarantine."

A loud scream was heard, and Sue's head spun toward the glass door of the lab. She could see the blood splatter on the glass becoming larger as one screaming woman continued to slam her head into the door repeatedly. Sue turned her head back to the projection to see Dr. Connors staring off again. Slowly, Sue's head turned back to the door and she said, "They turned."

Dr. Connors closed his eyes. "It did something to them. We did something to them." Connors' eyes opened and he took off his glasses. "The vaccine didn't prevent the virus; it just slowed the process and mutated the strain. We were prepared for it not to work or even for a few random deaths, but not for what it created. They are faster, smarter, and far more bloodthirsty than anything we have seen so far and..." Dr. Connors stopped and stared into the camera before softly saying, "I'm becoming one of them."

Dr. Brooks put her hand over her mouth and shook her head.

"No," she said softly and, as if he were standing there among them, Dr. Connors responded,

"Yes, love. I'm truly sorry. I'm sorry for what I've created, for what we've done. Above all else, I'm sorry I left you alone in this world." Tears fell from Dr. Connors's hazel eyes as he whispered, "If you're listening to this, Maxine, I love you and you need to run."

The projection stopped and Dr. Brooks's hands dropped from her face as she started screaming, "No, no! There has to be more! There has to be more!"

Sue quickly tucked her gun behind her back and walked up to Dr. Brooks. She fought it at first, but once Sue's arms wrapped around the doctor, she broke down crying on Sue's shoulder.

"It's okay. It's okay," Sue said and looked over at the Briggs boys. "Get Zero ready."

Sue looked back into the doctor's tearful eyes as she asked, "How do we get to the roof?"

Dr. Brooks pointed over to a metal door. "There's an elevator."

She started to clear away her tears and fix her glasses. For months, she had to have answers and solutions while the rest of the world panicked. Dr. Brooks had to think ahead while the rest of the world got to mourn. For the first time in a long time, she got to fall apart.

"Thank you," she said softly.

It felt odd, to be thanked for being around. A hug wasn't a life changing action, neither was opening a door, but, in this new world, the little actions were all that were left.

Dr. Brooks' keycard tapped a black pad and, within an instant, the metal door slid open. There was a long hallway with bright lights shining from above, bouncing off the white floors and walls. At the end of the hallway was a silver door. It was their ticket to freedom.

Sue looked at the Dr. Brooks and said, "We'll take you to the roof and then we're gonna get the others. So, I need you to swear on Dr. Connors' soul, that you'll wait for us."

Dr. Brooks was looking back at the bloody white lab coat

that covered Connors's body. She didn't answer; she didn't even pull her eyes away.

"Hey!" Sue shouted.

Dr. Brooks nodded. "I swear," she said softly. She started walking toward the pail of Infected as she said, "Just give me a moment to say goodbye."

Peter's hand went out and lightly cradled Dr. Brooks's head. She pulled away and turned to him. "I'll be right behind you guys."

Sue nodded. "All right."

Peter and Jordan rushed Patient Zero's bed along the bloodstained floor. The wheels of the hospital bed made an intense metal rattle as they scooted through the doorway. The Briggs boys rushed along with it and, after taking one last look at the Doctor, Sue followed behind.

Running down the long hallway behind the Briggs boys, Sue pulled the gun from behind her back to keep it from falling and started to run faster.

"Let's get him to the..." Sue's words were cut short as the bed came to a stop. The red LED lights of the elevator started to blink as numbers quickly started to count up.

Then they stopped.

The air was still as the silver doors started to open. Sue's eyes brightened up as the doors slid apart.

Then the white lights were replaced by red blinking lights. An alarm sounded and Specks' voice broke through the noise.

"Self-destruction in ten minutes."

"Oh, come on!" Peter screamed.

15

THE WAVE OF MURDER

PLANET DEAD

"*W*hy?" Catherine's whisper ran over the blood and leaped past Robert's lifeless body into Tennessee's ears. The pain that was buried inside of that hushed sound washed over Tennessee as the corners of her mouth started to rise up like to pink peaks, creating a haunting smile.

"You really don't know do you?" Tennessee asked.

She gave her boot a quick twist, grinding Catherine's fingers into the cement floor, before taking a step back and laughing.

"This is too fucking good," Tennessee said.

She leaned over to grab Catherine's weapon. She kept her eyes locked on Catherine, that and the barrel of her riffle never lost sight of Catherine.

"When we first locked eyes in that fucking tent, I thought for sure you recognized me." Tennessee leaned on the wall looking down at Catherine as she started to sling the spare weapon over her shoulder.

"Then, when you started going on and on about saving your little girlfriend, I thought, 'she really doesn't remember me'."

Catherine's hand slowly started to come back to her chest;

she bit her lip to fight back against the pain that was rushing through her body. A warm stream of blood was steadily making its way from her shoulder to the cold ground.

Catherine closed her eyes and took a deep breath as she started to get to her knees, but, before she could get up, she felt the wind rush out of her lungs as Tennessee's boot slammed into the middle of Catherine's chest, sending her flying back onto Robert's body.

Catherine's body twitched as she heard footsteps making their way toward her.

"I can't blame you, I guess. I was just a passing moment in your life, while you..." The sound of the footsteps came to a stop and Catherine listened as Tennessee slowly started to lean over her. "Mrs. Briggs, well you were my whole world. The only fucking light in the darkness. Do you know what—"

Catherine's boot went flying upwards until she heard the bone-chilling sound of Tennessee's jaw locking shut from the pressure of her combat footwear.

Tennessee stumbled back a few steps, her free hand going to stop the blood that was gushing from her mouth. Her tongue moved around until she felt the sharp sting and tasted the metallic liquid rushing from the deep gash left in her cheek.

Tennessee spit out a mouthful of blood and spotted the big chunk of meat that was once her inner cheek. Her eyes didn't come up fast enough to see Catherine rushing for her, with her shoulder lowered, but she felt it when Catherine's body connected with Tennessee's midsection, sending both women flying toward the ground.

The metal click clack of the rifles filled the room before Tennessee's chilling scream overpowered it.

"You fucking bitch!"

The two rolled back and forth with Tennessee's rifle tightly pressed between them. Catherine's hands locked onto the weapon as she rolled Tennessee onto the floor. Both women pulled and tugged, trying the free the rifle from the other's grasp. Yet, Tennessee was quickly getting the better of Catherine, who was fighting her hardest as dark blood pushed from her shoulder and dropped onto Tennessee's face.

Tennessee gave a quick pull and Catherine's head came flying forward into the concrete. A wave of black rushed over Catherine's eyes, but it was quickly overtaken by a sea of red as blood started falling from the wound on her head that had ripped open even more. The red flesh and blood made its grand appearance as Catherine just rested her head back on the cool floor. She stared up at the lights through her one open eye.

"Fuck!" Tennessee screamed out as she quickly wiped the blood from her lip and pointed the rifle at Catherine for the second time. "You, dumb bitch." Her finger softly rested on the trigger. "You got any last words?"

A whisper fell from Catherine's lips as Tennessee stood still with her rifle aimed at Catherine's head.

"What!" Tennessee screamed.

Catherine closed her eye as she shouted out, "I'm gonna kill you!"

Tennessee smiled. "You already did that, Mrs. Briggs."

Catherine's eye slowly started to open back up as Tennessee asked, "Do you believe in fate?"

Tennessee waited for an answer and then she smiled and spat out a bit of blood.

"I didn't. I spent 8 years in a cell thinking bad shit just happens to people. No God. No Devil and no divine master plan."

Tennessee kicked at Catherine's foot, causing the woman to look over at her.

"8 years thinking life was just a shit show and then that sack came off my head and I saw the light for the first time in my life," Tennessee said softly before looking over at Robert. "Fate gave me a second chance at evening the score."

Catherine's head dropped down to the floor. "If you're gonna kill me, then just kill me! You psycho bitch!"

With that last word, a ringing started in Catherine's head. She closed her eyes to keep the room from spinning.

Tennessee shook her head and raised the rifle pointing the barrel into the air.

"No," Tennessee said softly before stepping over Catherine and gathering up the other two rifles.

"A bullet's too good for you. I spent 8 years in hell. I might not be able to guarantee that kind of pain for you, but I can make fucking sure you don't die fast." Tennessee started walking toward the door, smiling. "You can sit there and think about how you raped me of my childhood, how you fucked up my life." Tennessee turned around slowly with her rifle pointed and the other two hanging off her shoulder.

"Sit here losing what's left of your mind, wondering what I'm gonna do to that little bastard of yours," Tennessee said.

Her words pulled Catherine's head to the side, forcing the woman to push herself to her knees.

"Please," Catherine said as blood trickled down her face.

Tennessee stood there staring at Catherine as she extended her hand out to Tennessee. Catherine's pleading creating an even bigger smile on Tennessee's face.

"Please?" Tennessee put her finger to her chin and nodded slowly. "I think I remember that word." Tennessee laughed and dropped her hand, pushing open the door behind her. "I remember crying and screaming, 'Please Mrs. Briggs, Please! I didn't do it!'"

Tennessee turned around and started walking through the doorway.

"Please! Tennessee please!" Catherine screamed.

As the footsteps started getting further and further away,

Catherine's chest began to tighten. She could feel her head starting to pound with each beat of her heart and, as Tennessee stepped through the doorway, Catherine did something she hadn't done in years, something she didn't recall ever doing.

"Help! Somebody Help!" She screamed for help.

Tennessee turned around slowly, smiling as she let the words fall from her bloody lips. "My name is Tiffany Myers!"

Catherine's eyes locked on Tennessee's face and for the first time she saw it, the same hazel eyes as that little girl who once cried in her office. She could see the same dark waves in Tennessee's hair as she saw that day, when she told that little girl she couldn't help her. When she turned her away to face whatever fate the world had for her.

"Tiffany." Catherine let the word fall from her lips.

Tennessee's eyes locked with Catherine as her fingers wrapped around the metal of the door and she screamed out, "And no one's ever gonna help you!"

With those words, the door slammed, and Catherine was left there...

With the blood...

With the pain...

With the dead.

16

A STRUGGLE FOR SURVIVAL

PLANET DEAD

"Ten minutes," Specks voice echoed through the hallway.

The lack of remorse in it sent a cold chill through Sue's body; she put her hand on the metal of the bed and softly said to herself as she watched the blinking red lights.

"We have to get out of here."

The white light of the elevator added a glow to the blood and bruises that had taken over Tennessee's body. She held her weapon tightly in her hands as she took in the sight of it all. The flashing red lights, the panic on their faces. It was all unfolding in slow motion for Tennessee as the voices in her head debated back and forth...

Kill them...

No! Lie to them...

No! Kill Them!

Tennessee's hand went to her head and she screamed out, "Shut that thing up!"

Sue's head spun back around toward the bright lights of the elevator.

The hall lights went out and a blood-covered Tennessee

glistened under the glow of the elevator lights. The hall lights turned red and Tennessee stood there, her head hung low and her eyes rested on her rifle.

Sue's lips parted as she attempted to speak, but her words were stolen from her and delivered in a small package as Jordan said, "Where's my mom and dad?"

Tennessee stood there, staring at the black metal of her rifle as that question pushed past the ringing of the alarm and the voices that were going off in her head.

Kill them!

She closed her eyes and held the handle of the rifle tighter in her hand as she said, "I'm sorry."

"Sorry? What the fuck you mean by sorry?" Peter shouted.

Tennessee took a few steps back into the elevator and leaned on the cool metal wall. Her bloody hand rested on the shiny silver as she softly said, "It was all my fault."

Sue's eyes found their way to Jordan, she watched as his head started to shake.

"What happened?" Sue shouted.

"We got surrounded..." Tennessee softly said. "A shit ton of things were down there. They had them locked up, but the shit ain't hold and we were fighting for our lives." Tennessee's eyes went over to Jordan and she shook her head as she said, "You're parents didn't make it, kid."

"No," Jordan whispered to himself. He started to back up, one foot following the other as his whisper turned into a scream, "No!" Then a roar, "NO!"

All he had, all he was fighting for was gone in an instant.

Peter rushed over to his nephew and took hold of him. He shook Jordan, forcing the boy to look at him. Jordan's eyes were drowning in tears now and just the sight of them caused Peter's eyes to do the same.

Peter put his hand on the back of Jordan's neck and said,

"Cry tomorrow and fight today, remember? We'll cry tomorrow, but we've got to keep fighting for them."

The little boy shook his head as his lips parted and his heart forced the words out between sobs. "I can't! I can't fight anymore." Jordan dropped to his knees and said, "I don't got anymore fight left in me."

Peter's arms wrapped around his nephew and held him close. Between the sobs and the alarm, Peter heard frantic footsteps speeding toward them.

Dr. Brooks came to a stop just short of slamming into Sue. "What the hell are you all waiting for!" Brooks screamed out, swinging a black bag toward the elevator as she pointed. "Get to the fucking chopper!"

Sue spun around quickly and let her fist fly connecting with the Doctor's jaw. Dr. Brooks fell back onto her ass and the black leather bag dropped to the floor. Something bloody and grey started rolling out of it; it bounced and tumbled until it landed at Sue's dirty white sneakers.

"Nobody got time for this shit!" Peter shouted.

Sue leaned over slowly, staring down at the bloody gray ball; she kicked it softly and watched as the bloody head fell to the side to reveal jet black eyes sunken into leather gray skin, with bloody red cracks running along his face.

Sue's hand went out to touch Dr. Connors's head, but it was snapped up quickly and shoved back into Dr. Brooks's bag. The woman stared up at Sue, then her head snapped toward Peter who was holding Jordan. They were all staring at the doctor as she slowly got to her feet.

"That's his head," Sue whispered.

Dr. Brooks pushed past Sue and slammed the bag onto the chest of Patient Zero, who was blissfully unaware of all the madness unfolding around him. Dr. Brooks' hands slapped onto the metal frame of the hospital bed as she started pushing it toward the elevator.

"That's his fucking head!" Sue screamed and grabbed Dr. Brooks's arm.

The doctor ripped loose and continued pushing as she shouted, "We have no time for me to give you a Virology 101 class!"

The wheels of the bed jumped as they pushed over the metal track of the elevator. Tennessee jumped to the side seconds before Dr. Brooks could slam the bed into her. The two of them stared at each other for a moment before Dr. Brooks looked over her shoulder at Peter.

"There's no turning back now."

Peter looked over at Sue then down at Jordan as he started to stand pulling the boy to his feet.

"We gotta go," he said.

Peter looked over to Sue again. His eyes were fighting back the tears, his mind was pushing back the thoughts, and his heart was fighting back the pain. "We all need to go."

Sue looked over at the elevator. She shook her head slowly but then felt a small hand take hold of hers. Sue's eyes went down to Jordan's water filled gaze as he softly said, "We need you."

Sue's free hand went up and she cleared away the tears from her eyes. There was no use crying about it, Catherine would have told her that. Sue's world had changed again, but tears weren't gonna save her.

Tears wouldn't bring back Catherine and Robert.

Tears weren't gonna help Jordan.

Sue held the boy's hand tightly and looked over at Peter, who was holding Jordan's other hand. The three of them went walking toward the bright white light of the elevator.

Three souls that lost far more than they ever thought they would...

Three souls that now only had each other.

17

THIS STORY BECOMES MORE GHASTLY

PLANET DEAD

The tall grass towered over her body.

She couldn't move.

She just stared up at the blue sky until his black hair and soft brown skin came into view.

He stood there with roses in his hands as he stared down at her.

"I'll miss you, Mom." Jordan's soft voice washed over her still body.

She was fighting to raise her hand to him, but all she felt was pain rushing through her. The blue skies turned black with a bright burst of lighting as a hand came out and rested on Jordan's shoulder. Tennessee came into view; she was wearing a long black dress and a large black hat. Jordan tossed the flowers onto Catherine's chest; it was then that she noticed the black suit he was wearing.

The ground started to shake, and she felt herself falling deeper into the earth as Tennessee smiled and screamed out, "We'll all miss you, Mrs. Briggs!"

The ground shook harder and Catherine shot up, screaming, "No!"

She looked around, but all she saw was darkness. For a moment, she questioned if she had a dream or if she truly was trapped in her own grave. The ground continued to shake, and something came crashing down beside her. She heard a loud thump and then felt something warm splash onto her face.

The ground became still, and then she heard them.

Ear-splitting screams came from beyond the darkness. She went to move her right arm, but a sharp pain rushed over her, causing Catherine to bite down on her lip.

She closed her eyes and it all quickly came back to her.

"Tiffany," she said softly.

A frantic pounding at the door caused her head to spin around in the darkness.

The pounding grew louder and was joined by screeches that raced through the darkness.

Catherine pulled her knees to her chest as her left hand ran along her leg down to her boot.

The metal door came flying off its hinges and a pack of grey-faced beings stood there, blood dripping from their lips. Flames from the explosion shined a light into the darkness to reveal that Robert's head had been crushed by a large metal pipe that had fallen from the ceiling.

Water and blood was running along the floor. The mixture rushed over Catherine's black boots. She stood there, her bloody right arm hanging useless while she wielded a double-edged blade in her left hand. The glow of the flames and Robert's blood covered her from head to toe. She was staring into a hoard of black eyes.

Catherine's lips slowly curled into a smile as she screamed, "Bring it on, motherfuckers!"

The End

If You Enjoyed This Book Please Leave A Review
&
Tell A Friend

18

BONUS STORY: PLANET DEAD 2: CHAPTER 1

PLANET DEAD

January 16, 2019 2:43 AM

Hello! I will be your narrator for this Telenvela

"Give me the fucking keys!" Christian shouted.

Christian's voice echoed through the empty mall parking deck. All eyes fell upon him as he stared down a salt and peppered haired old man. Their dark green eyes locked and through his gray beard Christian's father.

Jorge, smiled, "Wanna say that again, Mijo?" Jorge asked.

"Dee, come on. We're leaving." Christian said.

His hand went out toward the little boy. It wasn't easy being in the middle but it was a time long tradition for the Fidel family. Jorge was in the middle of his parents, Christian was the wall that protected his mother and Dominic was a little trophy, whoever he left with was clearly right and they knew best. Dominic slowly released the car door and ran over to his brother's side.

The driver door slammed making a chilling Wack that ran through the parking deck. Jorge stormed over to his sons and with him came the gut turning scent of tequila that flooded Christian's senses. His father grabbed Dominic by the arm and pulled the boy back. What started as a guy's night out at the Movie Tavern, turned into Jorge vs Jose Cuervo. Four Margaritas, five beers and three shots later, Jose was victorious. This left the Fidel boys with the task of trying to rip the car keys from Jorge's balled up fist.

"Oh, so you wanna play Papi, now!" Jorge's fingers tightened around Dominic's small arm.

Christian knew in the morning he would sober up and apologize, swear he didn't mean it, but in this moment the pain was warranted, it told Dominic never to cross him.

"You think you're better than me?" Jorge asked.

Christian's hands shot forward and he pushed his father back. The whole event felt like it was being recorded in slow motion, so Christian could watch it over and over again in his nightmares. The old man tripped over his own feet and fell face first into the cement. The boys ran toward their father only to be greeted by a back hand to Dominic's face. It all stopped then. Their hearts, their breathing, and time itself.

"Mijo," Jorge said softly. Dominic fell back into his older brother's arms. Jorge quickly stumbled to his feet, "I'm sorry-"

"No! Not tonight! You don't get to keep fucking up and apologizing!" Christian shouted.

The two stared at one another for a moment and then Jorge nodded his head. Red slowly took over Dominic's light brown skin but the boy was more focused on the tears building up in his father's eyes than he was with his own pain.

Jorge turned around with the keys jiggling in his hand. He got a few steps closer to the car before he looked back at Christian and said, "All the classes and all the college friends in the world isn't gonna make you better than me, Mijo." Jorge said. Jorge jumped into the car and started it up. The window came down and Jorge laughed, "You ain't better. No matter what you do. No matter how you dress it up, you're always just gonna be my boy."

The tires gave off a screeching sound. Christian and Dominic watched as the grey smoke filled the parking deck and their father's red tail lights blazed through the night.

"He's wrong." Dominic said. Christian looked down at his little brother. His hand went over the boy's cheek and Dominic asked, "You know that right?"

Christian leaned down and turned his back toward his little brother. "Come on, I'll carry you until we get to the sidewalk and then you're walking." Christian said with a smile. The little boy leaped onto his brother's back and the two went walking off into the darkness of the night.

"Why y'all always gotta fight?" Dominic asked.

They had been walking and randomly talking for about an hour before Dominic decided to dive head first into the real topic of the evening.

"Because he's a drunk." Christian said softly. Dominic went running forward and kicked a soda can into the air.

"He's always been a drunk. You think you'd be used to it by now." Dominic said.

"That's not the kind of life I wanna get used to and it's not the kind of life you need to get used to." Christian replied.

Dominic turned around and shrugged his shoulders, "He loves us, right?"

Christian sighed, "It ain't about that, it's about-"

Christian's words were cut short by the red and blue lights that were flashing in the distance. Dominic turned around to see what had grabbed his brother's attention. The little boy started racing down the sidewalk. Christian's hand went out to grab his little brother but Dominic was far from his grasp.

"Dominic!" Christian shouted.

He chased after his brother and every few feet that Christian got, the street lights would flicker. He could see the grey hoodie swinging back and forth as Dominic raced toward the red and blue lights.

"Dominic!" Christian hollered and the boy stopped at the end of the sidewalk.

Christian's hand grabbed his brother's hoodie and the streetlights went completely out. All Christian could see was the red and blue glow of the police cars. Dominic pulled away and pointed at the twisted smoking metal that seemed to fuse with the darkness of the streetlight pole. Christian couldn't tell where the car stopped and the light began. Yet, even with the twisted black metal and the bloody windshield, Christian knew just what he was staring at.

"You could have stopped him." Dominic said.

"No." Christian replied.

"You could have saved him."

"No."

"You killed him!" Dominic shouted.

Christian's eyes shot open and his body was fighting to breathe. He rolled over to his side in the darkness. His hand went over his sweaty chest. His heart seemed to be mirroring his original reaction from that fateful night. Yet, that was weeks ago.

Just a dream. Christian thought. He swung the cold wet covers off of his legs and stood up slowly. Life was never amazing or easy for Christian and the rest of the Fidel clan. His grandpa worked hard to get Christian's parents in America. Once they got there they all worked hard. Christian's father had two jobs right up until his accident. But, a hard working man doesn't really make a perfect man. Jorge was held down by his vices, mostly the liquid kind. Christian asked his Mother why his father drank so much and all she could say, was 'some people run from life in different ways.' But no matter what, life always catches up to you.

"Can't sleep?" Christian's mother, Gloria, asked.

The golden brown haired woman sat at the kitchen table with her cup of coffee and her DVRed telenovelas playing softly in the background. She asked the question without even turning to look at her son. Christian leaned in the doorway and sighed,

"Just needed some water." He said and Gloria nodded looking over at him.

"Seems like you got enough water pouring off of you." She said.

Christian looked down at his shirtless self and rolled his eyes, "Maybe if someone would turn on the AC-"

"When you pay the bills then we can talk about turning on the AC. Until then I hope you don't think I'll be washing your sheets everyday. I ain't done that since you were four and I don't plan on starting back up again." Gloria said with a laugh.

Christian pulled out a seat next to her and dropped down into it. "I suffered from night terrors." Christian said.

"Night terrors? Jesus, you pissed the bed because your father let you watch that movie, with the gringo that had knives for fingers." Gloria replied and waved her hand putting an end to the conversation.

There were two forms of waves from Gloria, one was the stop talking I'm watching my stories wave, and the other was your full of shit. Christian wasn't too sure which he got but he went with the former and stared at the tv with his mother.

The pair sat there in silence before Gloria softly said, "If you wanna talk about-"

"I don't." Christian quickly replied.

"I'm just saying, you shouldn't keep pushing everyone-"

"I don't wanna talk about it Ma."

Gloria put up her hands and nodded, "Okay." she said

softly. Christian leaned back in his seat and sighed, "So, you're going into work today?" Gloria asked.

Christian nodded and then ran his hands over his face, clearing away the warm salty sweat that still clung to his skin.

"Vince said one of the temps called out and he needs me to help Hector setup for the party." He said.

Gloria nodded and stood up slowly, "I don't see why that fool can't do it himself. He has two hands and two fucking legs like the rest of us." Gloria said.

Christian laughed, "He's the boss, Ma." Christian said with a smile and Gloria quickly turned off the tv before walking into the darkness of the hallway.

"He's an asshole that's what he is." Gloria replied.

The small wooden table creaked when Christian pushed himself to his feet. His eyes fell upon the darkness of the living room. He could make out the large hump that was his father's chair, placed off to the corner by the window.

"Back to the real world." Christian said and hit the light switch in the kitchen sending the rest of the house into darkness.

~

"*T*he question isn't if we should get involved, but why the hell haven't we?" The black dial on the radio spun and static took over the car.

"The wall was not only a good idea, but a great idea! It's keeping us and them saf-" Another flick of the finger sent the egotistical voices of the media into the dark world of static.

Christian didn't care much for the news these days. Every story was about death or someone thinking they knew what was best for everyone else. Protesting, shootings, twitter wars, it was all just noise to him and all he really wanted was silence. But in this world, that was only a luxury for the dead.

The dial came to a stop and the Mexican flair of Snow Tha Product filled Christian's ears. Music and art were becoming a Christian's personal safe space. Long nights of rap, reggaeton and painting were taking over Christian's life, but it kept him from facing the real monsters in his world. All the questions that seemed to haunt him when he closed his eyes.

Was it my fault?

Why didn't I stop him?

Why couldn't I save him?

Christian needed something to drown out the constant heckles of his internal monsters, but while music and art were amazing forms of escape, they didn't pay the bills. The car came to a slow stop between the white lines of the parking space. Christian rested his head back for a moment and closed his eyes as he let the battle cries of Snow wash over him. A deep sigh left Christian's lips and he opened his eyes to see a pale hairy set of butt-cheeks pressed against the driver side window.

"What the fuck!" Christian shouted and pushed open the car door sending the jiggling butt-cheeks flying into a nearby car.

Laughter filled the air as the man pulled up his large pants and spun around, "You've been away so long, I thought you might have missed this beautiful ass." Hector said smiling.

The two cousins stared at each other, Christian with a stone cold glare and Hector with a jolly smile. The moment faded as Christian laughed and turned off the car.

"No one on this planet could miss that fat ass." Christian said.

"That's offensive. We of the belly diverse community prefer round ass or a tasteful peach shaped emoji. I know you missed all the HR meetings but you really should be careful how you address your co-workers." Hector said.

Christian rolled his eyes, "Shut up. How much work you get done on the room?"

"Man, it's almost done, it just needs your magical tou-"

"You haven't even started, have you?" Christian asked.

"I haven't done shit since you left. I'm surprised I still have a job." Hector said.

The two laughed as they made their way to the employee entrance of the hotel. The Eastman Hotel was a bright new star to the city of Austin. Built during the Mayor's *'Make Austin Great Again'* campaign, it and a flock of new businesses opened up in the culturally appropriate, but far from politically correct, neighborhood of Little Tijuana.

It was an attempt to ease the heated tension growing in the Spanish community as Texas took up the major responsibility of building the now infamous 'Southern Grand' a wall that divided the United States from Mexico and the rest of South America. The addition of the Eastman and other businesses was a way for the city to say 'Yeah we're kicking out your friends and loved ones. Oh and cutting you off from your family back home but look at all the new jobs we made.' While it was a slap in the face of those fighting the good fight, it was still a job and one that paid pretty damn well, for just a few hours of setting up tables and chairs for rich people.

"How you and Tia doing?" Hector asked softly as he waited for Christian to punch in for work.

The computerized beep rang in Christian's ear as he stared at Hector through the little employee mirror that sat on the wall. The faded black sticker said *'smile, you don't know who's watching'*

"My father, who happens to be her husband is dead and Dominic is in a-coma, so I'm guessing we're not doing too hot these days." Christian said. Hector's eyes fell to the floor and Christian sighed, "Sorry, I'm just sick of everyone asking me that." Christian turned around and put his hands on the top of his head as he arched his back, "I mean Dee's in the hospital and Pop's in the ground. Me and Ma are just trying to stay above water, you know?" he said.

Hector nodded and stepped forward to the computer, "I understand that. I just don't know what to say or do." Hector said.

"Yeah, you and me both." He said.

Christian eyes floated over to the announcement board and a faint smile crept onto his face. It was an odd feeling, one he hadn't felt for weeks now, but the sight of her even in the form of an employee mugshot, got his heart beating uncontrollably. "Trinity won employee of the month again?" he asked.

Hector's head turned toward the board and he sighed, "Yeah, I was campaigning with the house keepers to get in the running this month, but then Vince wrote me up for hanging out in the housekeeping department during work hours." Hector rolled his eyes, "Bastardo." He said and then started walking down the hall towards the office.

Christian followed behind and as their uniformed grey shirts and black pants came closer to the end of the hall they could see Vince standing by his door looking at his watch. "And so it begins." Christian said softly.

"You two are late!" Vince said.

"No we're not, you said be here at ten." Christian replied.

"I did, but then I told Hector to let you know, we need to be here at seven if we're gonna get this done in time." Vince said.

All eyes fell onto Hector and the round man smiled, "Hey, Christian. We need to be in at seven because-" Hector, was cut off by Vince's over dramatic sigh. Hector did his best not to laugh at his boss, but the man was almost half of Hector's size in height. Which reminded Hector of the orange men that ran around in that chocolate factory movie. The thought of their green hair tossing back and forth as they sang made Hector smile until he felt an elbow in his ribs. His head turned toward

Christian who was giving him the best 'act right, motherfucker' look that he could muster.

"You two need to be more professional. You're always showing up late, always calling out." Vince said, he shook his head and then looked over at Christian, "This is your first day back. I don't want to have to write you up." he said.

Christian nodded and looked over at the door leading into the ballroom, "Sorry, just give me the floor plan and I'll make sure it gets done before tonight."

"It's not like you have any other choice than to get it done before tonight. The fucking party is tonight." Vince said. Hector looked over at Christian whose eyes were in the process of drilling a fiery hole into Vince's head.

Hector's arm went over his cousin's shoulder and he smiled, "Olvidare de este chico blanco," Hector said.

"What was that?" Vince asked.

"I said we got a lot of work ahead of us." Hector said with a smile. Christian nodded and walked off towards the ballroom. His steel toed black boots hit the ugly grey and black carpet, that had yellow swirl designs running throughout it. The mish-mash combination gave you the feeling of being drunk, fighting to walk down an ugly tilted hallway. Hector walked into the empty ballroom with the floor plans in hand. "You good?" he asked.

"Yeah, I'm straight. I just need a minute. I'll be back, I'm gonna go take a leak." Christian said and walked through the massive ballroom toward the hotel lobby. The wooden doors pushed open and the chill of the hotel air conditioning hit the back of Christian's neck. Images of Vince's face being slammed into the office door repeatedly flashed through Christian's head. The thoughts took up so much of his focus that he didn't see the teenage boy in front of him, until he almost knocked him over. "Whoa, sorry man." Christian said with a smile. The boy stared at Christian and stepped back blocking the doorway to the bathroom. "You playing bathroom bouncer?" Christian asked.

"My dad's in there. He needs privacy," The boy said and Christian nodded.

"That doesn't sound suspect at all." Christian said with a mocking grin to the boy. "Is daddy day drunk or something?" he asked.

"No." the boy said and glared.

"Jeremy who are you talking to?" A male voice echoed through the bathroom. Christian's eyes went from the boy to the white tile walls of the bathroom.

"Sorry sir, but you can't close the bathroom off for your own personal use." Christian said.

A gray haired man in a cotton white button up shirt stepped from around the corner. His icy blue eyes glared at Christian for a moment, "Yeah well my wife isn't feeling too good and she rushed into the wrong restroom, I didn't want-" The man's words came to a cold stop as Christian pointed at a dark red spot on his white shirt.

"Is that blood?" Christian asked.

The man's eyes went down toward his shoulder and then they shot back to Christian, "Yeah, I cut myself on your fucking bathroom stall." The man said. Christian looked at Jeremy and then back at the man.

"I'll call security, so you can file a report with the hotel."

"No, that's fine. Everything is fine, I'm just waiting on-" The man smiled as his pale blonde haired wife slowly stumbled her way out of the bathroom. She fell into her husband's arms.

"Holy shit, are you okay?" Christian asked.

"I'm fine, I'm fine." The woman replied with a faint smile, "Don't ever eat airport sushi." Her husband smiled and slowly eased her onto her feet.

"Come on sweetie, let's get you to the room," the man said.

"Do you need any help?" Christian asked and the man

waved him off. Then shoved his hand into his pocket and pulled out a folded bundle of cash and held it out toward Christian.

"We're fine, thank you. She just needs to rest." The man said.

Christian stared at the folded twenties and tens and then looked back at the man, "I'm fine sir, really. I-"

"No, take it." The man insisted as he pushed the cash into Christian's hand. When Christian's eyes came up from the green paper it was just in time to see Jeremy looking back at him before disappearing around the corner toward the elevators. Christian looked down at the cash once again and shoved it into his pocket.

"White people are weird," he said softly to himself. When he turned the corner into the bathroom his hands shot up to defend his nose. While his skin acted as a gas mask and tightened around his nose to block the rancid smell of shit and vomit, there was nothing to save his eyes from the stinging sensation or the sight of the dark red that was slowly spilling out from under the stall door. Christian walked over toward the first stall and slowly pushed it open to see what he could only imagine would be a janitor's worst nightmare. The white toilet and walls were covered in dark red blood and bits of what Christian could only describe as chunks of meat.

"Security!" Christian frantically shouted through the halls as he ran from the bathroom.

ALSO BY SYLVESTER BARZEY

If you enjoyed this book please be sure to review it and tell a friend.

Don't worry the ride isn't over:

Planet Dead 2: Patient Zero

Planet Dead 3

Get Your Free Planet Dead Novel: Love Bites Today

More Books At:

Amazon

www.sylvesterbarzey.com/books

If that isn't enough zombie and horror madness for you, then become a "Survivor Among The Living" an all exclusive newsletter and secret website for zombie & horror lovers. Win prizes, read sneak peeks, and survivor the outbreak with Catherine and other like minded crazy people.

Join Today

Also join "Sylvester Barzey's Fan Club" for prizes, updates and a look inside the author's mind.

Join Today

Learn More At www.sylvesterbarzey.com

ABOUT THE AUTHOR

Sylvester Barzey is a father, a husband, a soldier, and an "**Anything Goes HORROR**" writer.

- *Missing Children*
- *Deadly Wives*
- *Haunted Baby Rattles*
- *A LOT OF DEAD BODIES!*
- *Vampires (That Don't Sparkle & Don't Believe In Dating Their Food Source! Would You Date A Cow?)*
- *Werewolves*
- *Zombies (A Whole Lot Of F#@king Zombies)*
- *Oh & Some Bad Words.*

He writes what he likes and what he likes is **HORRIFYING!**
Reach out to me by Author@sylvesterbarzey.com or visit his www.sylvesterbarzey.com

Made in the USA
Monee, IL
04 July 2021

72274429R00135